When Lane slowly re... ...,
it took a moment for ... ing at
her expectantly. "Um ....Lane," she finally
managed.

Forcing herself to move, she opened the screen door
and didn't stop until she was upstairs with her bedroom
door shut firmly behind her. As she leaned back against
it, she had to remind herself to breathe. Lane had more
raw sensuality in his little finger than most men had in
their entire bodies.

Her heart suddenly began to pound against her ribs.
When had she started thinking of him by his first name?
It had been much easier and a lot less personal to keep
him compartmentalized as Donaldson, her adversary—
the very man who stood between her and her goal of
owning all of the Lucky Ace.

* * *

Your Ranch...Or Mine? is part of
The Good, the Bad and the Texan series:
Running with these billionaires will be one wild ride.

* * *

If you're on Twitter,
tell us what you think of Harlequin Desire!
#harlequindesire

Dear Reader,

Something that you might not know about me or even suspect is that I not only write romance novels, but I'm also not a bad poker player. I'm not saying I'm ready to turn professional—far from it—but I am able to hold my own at a poker table in a game of Texas Hold 'Em. That's why I decided to make one of my heroes a professional poker player.

The third installment of The Good, the Bad and the Texan series, *Your Ranch...Or Mine?*, explores what happens when professional poker player Lane Donaldson wins 50 percent interest in the Lucky Ace Ranch. But when he meets his partner's granddaughter, Taylor Scott, and he challenges her to a poker game for complete ownership of the ranch, the stakes have never been higher.

So please sit back and enjoy Lane and Taylor's journey to their happily ever after in *Your Ranch...Or Mine?*. And, as always, I hope you love reading about them as much as I enjoyed writing their story.

All the best,

Kathie DeNosky

YOUR RANCH...
OR MINE?

—

KATHIE DeNOSKY

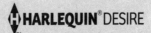

Recycling programs
for this product may
not exist in your area.

ISBN-13: 978-0-373-73312-5

YOUR RANCH...OR MINE?

Copyright © 2014 by Kathie DeNosky

Printed in U.S.A.

KATHIE DeNOSKY

lives in her native southern Illinois on the land her family settled in 1839. She writes highly sensual stories with a generous amount of humor; her books have appeared on the *USA TODAY* bestseller list and received numerous awards, including two National Reader's Choice Awards. Kathie enjoys going to rodeos, traveling to research settings for her books and listening to country music. Readers may contact her by emailing kathie@kathiedenosky.com. They can also visit her website, www.kathiedenosky.com, or find her on Facebook, www.facebook.com/Kathie-DeNosky-Author/278166445536145.

This book is dedicated to my poker playing friends Chris Doss, Jeremy Miller and Michele Hudson. Over the years I've had a ton of fun playing poker with you and hope we get to play again soon.

One

Lane Donaldson couldn't help but laugh as he watched the five men he called brothers acting like a bunch of damned fools.

It was funny how a baby could do that to otherwise intelligent grown men. And whether he wanted to admit it or not, he was no different. He had done his fair share of making faces and odd noises to try to get a smile out of the kid, as well.

He had invited his family and friends to the barbecue to celebrate his winning half of the Lucky Ace Ranch in a poker game last fall. But because of the birth of his nephew a few months back, the celebration had turned into a party to welcome the new baby to the family as well as to commemorate his big win.

"Y'all are going to scare the pudding out of little

Hank," Nate Rafferty complained as he made another face at the infant in his brother Sam's arms.

Nate and Sam were as different as night and day, even though they were the only two biological siblings out of the band of foster brothers who had spent their adolescence together on the Last Chance Ranch. While Sam was happily married with a three-month-old son, Nate was too busy trying to date the entire female population of the southwest to settle down. In fact, of the four remaining confirmed bachelors, Lane included, Nate was hands down the wildest of the bunch.

"And I suppose you think you're not scaring the kid with that sappy grin of yours, Nate?" Ryder McClain asked, laughing. "I play chicken with two thousand pounds of pissed-off beef every weekend and you're still enough to scare the hell out of me." A rodeo bull fighter, Ryder was without question one of the bravest men Lane had ever had the privilege of knowing—and Ryder was also the most laid-back, easygoing of his foster brothers.

"How much longer before you become a daddy, Ryder?" T. J. Malloy asked, taking a swig from the beer bottle in his hand. A highly successful saddle bronc rider, T.J. had retired at the ripe old age of twenty-eight and in the ensuing years had started raising and training champion reining horses.

"The doctor told us the other day that it could be just about any time," Ryder answered, glancing uneasily over to where his wife, Summer, sat talking to Sam's wife, Bria, and Bria's sister, Mariah. "And the closer it gets, the more I feel like a long-tailed cat in a room full of rocking chairs."

"Getting a little nervous, are you?" Lane asked, grinning.

"More like a lot," Ryder said, glancing again at his wife as if to assure himself she was still doing all right.

"I know exactly how you feel, Ryder," Sam said, nodding. "About a month before Bria had little Hank, I mapped out the quickest route to the hospital and made several practice runs just to be sure I could get her there in time."

"Both of you have helped cows during calving season for years," Nate said, his tone practical. "If you'd had to, you could have delivered little Hank, Sam. And you could deliver your and Summer's baby, Ryder."

Every one of them gave Nate an unimpressed look, then, shaking their heads, resumed their conversation.

"What?" Nate asked, obviously confused.

"I want the best for my wife when the time comes for her to have our baby and I'm man enough to admit I'm not it," Ryder answered, his disgusted expression stating louder than words what he thought of Nate's logic.

"Have you given in and asked the doctor if the baby is a boy or a girl, Ryder?" Jaron Lambert asked, staring across the yard at the women.

"We really don't care as long as the baby is healthy and Summer is okay," Ryder answered, shaking his head. "She wants to be surprised and I want whatever she wants."

"Well, I hope it's a girl," Jaron said flatly.

Lane couldn't help but chuckle. "Mariah still not talking to you, bro?"

Jaron shook his head. "She's still pissed off about what I said when Sam and Bria told us they were having a boy."

Jaron and Mariah had been arguing from the time they learned that Bria and Sam were expecting. Jaron had been sure the baby would be a boy, while Mariah had insisted it would be a girl. Apparently, Mariah had taken exception to Jaron's gloating after he'd been proven right.

"Yeah, women don't like it very much when a man says 'I told you so,'" Lane said, grinning.

"You think, Dr. Freud? I figured that out all by myself right after she stopped talking to me, genius." Jaron's sour expression and reference to Lane's psychology degree caused Lane to laugh out loud.

"When are you going to stop beating around the bush and take that girl out for a night on the town?" Lane asked.

"I've told y'all before, I'm too old for her," Jaron answered sullenly.

"That's bull and we all know it," T.J. shot back. "She's only eight years younger than you. It might have mattered when you were twenty-six and she was eighteen, but she's in her mid-twenties now. Your ages aren't that big a deal anymore."

"Yeah, and it's not like she wouldn't go," Ryder added. "She's had a crush on you from the time she met you. Although I can't for the life of me figure out why."

Taking a sudden interest in the tops of his boots,

Jaron shrugged. "It doesn't matter. I've got a world championship to win and I don't need the distraction." Competing in bull riding and bareback events, Jaron was a top contender to win the All-Around Rodeo Cowboy Championship for the third year in a row.

"While you guys try to talk some sense into Jaron, I see a lady who looks like she could use a trip around the dance floor," Nate said, grinning. "And I can't think of a man here who is better at doing the Texas two-step than me."

When they all turned to see which woman Nate was talking about, Lane felt as if he had taken a sucker punch to the gut. A little above average in height, the leggy redhead in question wasn't just pretty, she was absolutely breathtaking. Her long, straight, copper-colored hair complimented her creamy complexion to perfection and he couldn't help but wonder what it would feel like to run his fingers through the silky strands.

"Who is that?" T.J. asked, sounding as awestruck as Lane felt.

"I've never seen her before," Lane answered, looking around. It didn't appear she was with any of the other guests.

"She had to have just arrived," Nate added, sounding quite certain of the fact. "Otherwise, I would have noticed her before now."

As Nate started across the yard toward the woman, Lane couldn't say he was sorry she had decided to crash the barbecue he was throwing to celebrate winning half of the Lucky Ace Ranch. He would have thrown the party when he first became a partner in the place, but it had been so late in the fall he had decided to wait until spring, when it was warmer and they could celebrate Texas style—with an outdoor barbecue and dance. And now he was glad that he had. She was without question one of the prettiest women he'd ever seen and a welcome addition to the view in his ranch yard.

Lane frowned at the uncharacteristic stab of envy coursing through him as he watched Nate introduce himself to her, then take her in his arms to move around the temporary dance floor Lane's hired hands had installed for the festivities. He'd never been envious of any of his brothers before, but there was no denying that was exactly what was wrong with him at the moment.

When the country band took a break, Lane watched Nate talk with the woman for a moment before he shrugged and sauntered back to the group. The woman glanced at him and his brothers standing on the opposite side of the dance floor, then walked over to the refreshment table.

"It doesn't look like that went exactly the way you planned, Nate," T.J. said, laughing.

Looking as if he couldn't quite believe what had happened, Nate shook his head. "I must be losing my touch."

"Why do you say that?" Sam grinned. "Has she heard about your love-'em-and-leave-'em reputation?"

"No, smart-ass." Nate gave Sam a dark scowl before turning his attention to Lane. "All she did was ask me questions about *you*."

"Me?" It was the last thing Lane had expected to

hear. Why would she be inquiring about him? "What did she want to know?"

Nate shrugged. "She mainly wanted to know how long you've lived on the Lucky Ace and if you intend to stay here or sell out and move on." He frowned and glanced over his shoulder at the woman. "She didn't even know which one of us you were. I had to point you out."

Lane was more bewildered than ever as he stared across the yard at the woman surveying the array of food the caterer had prepared for his guests. He supposed she might have been in the gallery at one of the high-stakes poker tournaments he'd played over the years. But he rejected that idea immediately. If she had, she wouldn't have needed Nate to identify him.

"Looks like you might have an admirer, Lane," Ryder said, grinning like a six-year-old kid turned loose in a toy store.

"I doubt it," Lane answered, shaking his head as he stared across the yard at the woman. "If that was the case, she wouldn't have had to ask Nate about me."

His brothers all nodded their agreement as they continued to stare at her.

Deciding that he could speculate all evening and still not come up with any firm answers as to why the woman would be so curious about him, Lane took a deep breath. "No sense in standing here wondering about it. I'm going to ask her."

"Good luck with that," Jaron said.

"If you strike out like Nate, let me know and I'll give my luck a try," T.J. added, laughing.

Ignoring his brothers' teasing comments, Lane crossed the dance floor to the opposite side of the yard, where the woman had seated herself at an empty table. "Mind if I join you?" he asked as he pulled out a chair and started to sit down. "I'm—"

"I know who you are. You're Donaldson." She was silent for a moment, then, without looking up from her plate, shook her head. "You might as well join me. It wouldn't do me a lot of good if I told you that I did mind."

Her cool tone, obvious hostility and refusal to look directly at him caused him to hesitate. He was almost certain they had never met. What could he have possibly done to offend her? And why had she crashed his party just to give him the cold shoulder?

"Forgive me for not being able to recall, but have we met before?" he asked, determined to find out what was going on.

"No."

"Then why the chilly reception?" he asked pointblank as he pushed the chair back under the table without sitting down. He had no intention of sitting beside her when it was obvious she didn't want his company. But for the life of him, he couldn't figure out the reason for her attitude toward him.

"I'm here to discuss something with you and I'd rather not get into it in front of your guests," she said, pushing the food around on the plate in front of her with her fork. When she finally looked up at him, her emerald-green eyes sparkled with anger. "We'll talk after the party is over."

Lane studied her delicate features as he tried to get a read on what she might be up to. She had never met him before. She'd shown up to his party uninvited, and she was extremely angry with him. Now she was refusing to tell him why?

He had no idea what her agenda was, but it was more than a little apparent she had one. He had every intention of finding out what was going on, but she was right about one thing. Getting to the bottom of things would have to wait until the party started winding down. He wasn't about to ruin the rest of his guests' good time by getting into an argument with her now. And there was no doubt in his mind that an argument was exactly what was going to happen.

Nodding toward her plate, he gave her what he hoped, considering the circumstances, was a congenial enough smile. "I'll let you get back to your meal and I'll see you after the party."

As he turned to walk away, Lane checked his watch. Being a professional poker player for the past ten years, he'd long ago learned the fine art of patience. But it was sure as hell failing him now. He suddenly couldn't wait for the party to end so he could find out who the woman was and what she wanted. Then he'd send her on her way.

As Taylor Scott waited for the last of the guests to leave the barbecue, she gathered her anger around her like a protective cloak and reminded herself she was on a mission. Donaldson was a scheming, cheating snake in jeans. Villains in the old Western movies her grandfather used to watch always wore black hats and, quite appropriately, Donaldson's wide-brimmed Resistol was as black as his heart. But the one thing she hadn't counted on was how darned good-looking he would be.

Watching him bid farewell to an extremely pregnant woman and her husband, Taylor couldn't help but notice how tall he was, how physically fit. From his impossibly wide shoulders to his trim waist, long, muscular legs and big, booted feet, he had the body of a man who spent his days doing manual labor. Not the look she'd expected of someone who sat for endless hours at a poker table. But what had really thrown her off guard was the warmth and sincerity she'd detected in his chocolate-brown eyes. Framed with lashes as black as his hair, they were the kind of eyes a woman could feel safe getting lost in.

Taylor gave herself a mental shake. Donaldson might be Mr. Tall, Dark and Drop-Dead Gorgeous, but he wasn't a man who could be trusted any farther than she could pick him up and throw him. He was a con man, a swindler—a conniving thief. There was no way he could have won half of the Lucky Ace Ranch in a card game with her grandfather if he hadn't cheated. For over sixty years her grandfather had been considered one of the best players in the world of high-stakes professional poker, and he would never have risked any part of his ranch if he hadn't been certain he could beat the man.

"Let's go inside," Donaldson said when he reached the table where she was sitting.

"Why?"

She hadn't been inside her grandfather's home in several years and she worried her emotions would get the better of her when she walked into the house without him being there. That was something she would rather die than allow Donaldson to see.

He pointed to the catering staff as they cleaned up. "I thought my office might be a little more private." He shrugged. "But it's up to you how much privacy you think we need."

Grinding her back teeth over the fact that he'd called her grandfather's office *his,* Taylor pushed her chair back. She could deal with her feelings later—after she'd ousted the interloper.

"The office is fine," she said, rising to her feet. "I doubt that you'll want anyone to hear what I have to say anyway."

He stared at her for several long seconds before he nodded and stepped back so she could lead the way across the yard.

Taylor felt his gaze on her back as she walked up the steps and crossed the porch, but she ignored the little shiver of awareness that streaked up her spine. She had come to Texas for one reason. She was going to confront the man who had stolen part of her grandfather's ranch, buy it back, then take great pleasure in ordering him off the property.

But when she entered the kitchen, she forgot all about Donaldson and his disturbing gaze as emotion threatened to swamp her. Being in her grandfather's ranch house, knowing that he wasn't there and never would be again, was almost more than she could bear.

"The office is just down the hall and to your…"

"I know where it is," she snapped, cutting him off. To have a rank stranger try to direct her through a house that held the happiest memories of her childhood irritated her as little else could.

Her heart ached with unshed tears when she walked into her grandfather's office. How could everything look the same and yet be entirely different from the last time she was here?

"Please have a seat, Ms...."

"My name is Taylor Scott," she answered automatically.

Nodding, Donaldson motioned toward one of the two big leather armchairs in front of the desk. "Would you like something to drink, Taylor?"

The sound of his deep baritone saying her name caused an interesting little flutter in the pit of her stomach. She took a deep breath to regain her equilibrium and lowered herself onto the chair. "N-no, thank you."

He placed his hat on the credenza, then walked around the desk to sit in the high-backed chair. "What is it that you wanted to discuss with me?"

Maybe if she waited to reveal her identity she could get him to incriminate himself as having cheated her grandfather. "I'd like to know what you intend to do with your interest in the Lucky Ace," she stated, meeting his dark brown gaze head on.

She wasn't surprised when his expression remained unreadable. After all, he was a professional poker player and well practiced at keeping his emotions concealed.

"I'm not in the habit of discussing something of this

nature with a stranger," he said as if choosing his words carefully.

"I understand you won half of the ranch from Ben Cunningham." When he nodded, she went on. "I'm here to make you an offer for your share."

He slowly shook his head. "It's not for sale."

"Are you sure, Donaldson? The offer I'm willing to make is quite generous."

"Please, call me Lane," he said, giving her a smile that caused her heart to skip a beat. Several of Hollywood's leading men were among her clients. They'd spent thousands of dollars on dental and cosmetic surgery and still couldn't come close to having his perfect smile.

Giving herself a mental shake, she decided to focus on the fact that he was a swindler and ignore his good looks, as well as his request to call him by his first name. That was more personal than she cared to get with the man.

"I'm prepared to pay you well above market value if you can vacate the property within a week," she pressed.

"I'm quite happy here, and even if I weren't, I wouldn't consider selling my share of the Lucky Ace without consulting my partner first, and he's currently in California." He silently stared at her, as if analyzing the situation, before he spoke again. "Why do you think you want my share of the ranch?"

"I don't *think* I want the ranch. I *know* I want it," she said impatiently.

"Why?" he demanded. She could tell she was getting

to him when he sat forward, showing the first signs that he was becoming irritated with the situation.

Confident that she was gaining the upper hand, she couldn't help but smile. "Before we get into that, could I ask you a couple of questions, Donaldson?"

He stared at her for a moment before he answered. "You can ask, but I'm not guaranteeing that I'll give you the answers you want to hear."

"How did you manage to get Ben Cunningham to wager any part of this ranch in that poker game last fall?" she queried.

"Why do you think it was my idea that he use the Lucky Ace to cover his bet?" he asked, slowly leaning back in the desk chair.

"Are you saying he voluntarily put it up?" she shot back.

"Why do you think otherwise, Taylor?" he asked, sounding irritatingly calm.

She had heard that he was a licensed psychologist, and it seemed that the rumor was true. Instead of answers, he followed every one of her questions with one of his own—like any good therapist would do. Taylor decided right then and there that if he asked her how she felt about the situation, she was going to reach across the desk and bop him a good one.

"I happen to know that he wouldn't have wagered the ranch unless he was certain he had the winning hand," she stated flatly.

"So you know Mr. Cunningham?" he asked, his expression still as bland as dry toast.

"Yes, I know him quite well. But we'll get to that

later." She was getting nowhere fast and it infuriated her no end that Donaldson remained calm and collected when she was filled with nothing but frustration and anger. She was ready for a verbal battle, but he wasn't taking the bait. "What I'd like to know is why you're living here in his house."

"That's none of your business, Ms. Scott." Addressing her in a more formal way was the only outward indication he was losing patience.

"You've won several of the larger poker tournaments and I would think that with your wealth you would prefer something a bit more urban than a ranch house in the middle of nowhere," she said, hoping he would give her an indication of why he had taken up residence in her grandfather's home.

"Nice try, Taylor." To her surprise, a slow smile curved his mouth. "Now, why don't we start over and you tell me what you've been dancing around since we came in here?"

Deciding that he wasn't going to divulge anything without her telling him who she was, she took a deep breath. "I'm Ben Cunningham's granddaughter and I want to know how you got him to bet half of the ranch in that poker game, why you're staying here and what it will take to get you to sell your interest and get off the Lucky Ace for good."

"Since you're here grilling me, I take it that Ben hasn't supplied you with the answers to your questions?" he asked, raising one black eyebrow.

"No."

"I'm sure he has his reasons for not telling you, and

I'm not going to betray his trust." He shook his head. "But I can tell you that he suggested I move into the house to watch over the place while he was in California visiting with you and your parents."

"What about getting him to bet half of the ranch?" she demanded, not at all satisfied with his unwillingness to tell her what she wanted to know. "How did you manage that?"

"I had nothing to do with him putting up any part of the ranch. It was his idea and his alone," Donaldson answered.

"I have a hard time believing that, Donaldson." Unable to sit still any longer, Taylor rose to her feet to pace back and forth in front of the desk. "He bought this land sixty years ago with his first poker winnings. It was his pride and joy and when he and my grandmother married, they built this house and raised my mother here. In all that time, he never once considered risking any part of it. Why would he suddenly change his mind last fall?"

"You'll have to ask Ben." He smiled. "I haven't heard from him in a couple of months. How is your grandfather? Is he enjoying his time in sunny California? Has he mentioned when he'll be coming back to the ranch?"

Taylor stopped pacing and turned to face him. Her eyes burning with tears she refused to allow her nemesis to see, she took a deep, steadying breath. "Grandpa passed away about three weeks ago."

Donaldson's smile immediately disappeared. "I'm really sorry to hear that. Ben was a good man and the best poker player I've ever had the privilege to know. You have my deepest sympathy."

"T-thank you," she said, sinking into the armchair. Talking about her grandfather, knowing he was gone and that she had been powerless to stop the inevitable, was overwhelming.

"Here, drink this," he said, handing her a glass tumbler as he lowered himself into the armchair beside her.

Lost in her misery, she hadn't been aware that he'd risen from the chair behind the desk. "What is it?" she asked, looking at the clear liquid in the glass.

He gave her a sympathetic smile. "It's just water."

"Oh."

"How did Ben die?" he asked softly.

"He had a massive heart attack," she said woodenly. "He'd apparently known about his heart condition for quite some time, but didn't tell anyone. When I learned about it, I insisted that he see the top cardiologist in Los Angeles. But it was too late. He went into cardiac arrest the day before he was scheduled for open-heart surgery."

They sat in silence for some time before he commented. "I wonder why the poker federation failed to announce Ben's passing last week at the tournament in Vegas?"

Finishing the glass of water, she placed the tumbler on the desk. "It wasn't announced because they don't know about it. He asked that his death be kept quiet until after his ashes were scattered here at the ranch."

"Is that why you're here now?" he asked. "To tell me you're going to scatter Ben's ashes?"

"No." She determinedly met his questioning gaze. "I took care of his request yesterday evening at sunset."

He looked doubtful. "If you were here yesterday, why didn't I see you?"

"Because I know this place like the back of my hand," she answered. "There's a road two miles west of here that leads to the creek on the southern part of the ranch. Grandpa told me that if something happened to him he wanted his ashes released at sunset down by the creek where he asked my grandmother to marry him." She stared at her hands, clasped tightly in her lap. "I'm sure you can understand that it was a private moment for me."

"Of course," he said quietly.

Suddenly feeling drained of energy, she hid a yawn behind her hand. "Now that you know about my grandfather's death, there's no reason not to answer my questions." She gave him a pointed look. "Besides, I inherited the other half of the Lucky Ace Ranch and as the co-owner, that gives me the right to know everything. And the first thing I intend to find out is how you managed to swindle my grandfather."

Two

Lane stared at Taylor for several long seconds as he worked to control his anger. He was still trying to come to terms with losing a good friend, as well as his partner in the ranch. The last thing he wanted was to be defending his integrity. But it appeared that was exactly what he was going to have to do.

"Before this goes any farther, let me set you straight, Ms. Scott," he said, wondering how he could still find her attractive when he was angry enough to bite nails in two. "I have never been a cardsharp, nor will I ever be. I take my poker games very seriously and I can guarantee you that I don't have to cheat to win. I pit my skill against other players' and I'm good enough to be quite successful at it—just as your grandfather was."

"But he had more years of experience than you are

old," she insisted. "How could you possibly beat him unless the game was rigged?"

"I know this is probably hard for you to believe, but your grandfather and I had a lot in common," he stated. "We had a mutual respect for the game and for each other as worthy opponents. I'm sorry if you can't accept that I had the skill to beat your grandfather, but I wouldn't cheat at cards any more than Ben would have."

Suddenly needing a drink, he rose to his feet, walked over to the credenza and poured himself a shot of bourbon. Downing the amber liquid in one gulp, he let the warmth spread throughout his chest before he turned to face her.

"The day I won an interest in this ranch, I had the better hand." He shook his head. "We could have played another day and he might have come out the winner. That's the game and a chance you take any time you sit down at a poker table."

"I realize that there's always a risk of losing," she said, sounding a little less confident. She hid another yawn behind her delicate hand then continued, "But my grandfather was arguably the best poker player in modern history. He could tell at a glance what his odds of winning were and how much he could safely wager. He would have never bet half of the ranch if he hadn't been certain he would win."

"And because of his miscalculation that makes me guilty of cheating?" Lane demanded.

She yawned yet again. "He wouldn't have risked—"

"I think we've adequately covered that already," he interrupted. He took a deep breath in an effort to cool the fury burning in his gut. She wasn't listening and he was tired of beating his head against a brick wall trying to convince her of his innocence. "Look, it's past midnight and we're getting nowhere. Let's put this discussion on hold until tomorrow morning."

She stared at him for a moment before she finally nodded and rose to her feet. "That would probably be best."

"Where are you staying?" he asked. "I'll drive you to your hotel."

Looking suspicious, she asked, "Why?"

"You're too tired to be behind the wheel of a car," he stated flatly.

"I'm staying right here," she said, her stubborn tone indicating that hell would freeze over before she budged on the issue. Resigned, he followed her out into the hall.

"I'm assuming that you have a bedroom you used when you visited your grandfather?"

"My room is the one with the lavender ruffled curtains and bedspread at the opposite end of the hall from the master suite," she answered. She started toward the kitchen. "I'll just get my overnight bag from the car."

"Give me your keys and I'll get it for you," he said, holding out his hand.

Even though she had made him angry enough to want to forget his manners, he couldn't ignore the code of conduct his foster father had taught him and his brothers about how a man was supposed to treat a woman. When a woman had something that needed to be carried, a man stepped forward and took care of it for her—no matter how small or lightweight the object was. No excuses.

"I can get it," she insisted, taking a set of keys from the front pocket of her jeans.

He took them from her and tried to ignore the tingling sensation that streaked up his arm when he brushed her fingers with his. "You're tired and it's probably heavy," he said through gritted teeth. "Go on upstairs and I'll leave it outside your door."

"It's the blue backpack on the front passenger seat," she called after him as he left the house. She said something else, but instead of turning back to ask what it was, he continued on to the little red sports car parked by his truck.

At the moment, it was better to put a little distance between them. If he didn't, he couldn't be certain he wouldn't lose his temper and tell her what he thought of her and her ridiculous accusations—or grab her and kiss her until they both forgot that she was a lady and he was trying to be a gentleman.

He stopped short. Where had that thought come from? He would just as soon cozy up to a pissed-off wildcat than to get up close and personal with Taylor Scott. She might be one of the hottest women he'd seen in all of his thirty-four years, but she represented the kind of trouble that a man just didn't need.

Shaking his head at his own foolishness, he unlocked the Lexus and reached inside to get Taylor's backpack. The light, clean scent of her perfume assailed his senses and reminded him of just how long it had been since he'd lost himself in the charms of a willing woman. The scent only added an unwelcome element to the level of his frustration and he cussed a blue streak when his lower body began to tighten. And it didn't help matters one damned bit knowing she would be sleeping in the room directly across the hall from the one he had been using since moving to the ranch six months ago.

He clenched his teeth as another wave of heat surged through his body. How could he possibly feel this level of desire for a woman when she irritated the living hell out of him? For that matter, how had she managed to make him forget everything he'd learned in seven years of studying to become a psychologist?

He had known immediately that she was fishing for information and he'd successfully evaded answering her by turning the tables and asking questions of his own. He'd even found her interrogation mildly amusing. But what he couldn't quite come to terms with was the fact that when she'd started making accusations, he had let her get to him.

Lane had played poker with men who made it a point of talking smack in an effort to throw him off his game, and not once had he ever let any of it affect him. For one thing, he recognized the insults as a psychological ploy and simply tuned the men out. And for another thing, they all had better sense than to cross the line and accuse him of cheating. But when Taylor made it clear that she thought he had swindled her grandfather out of his ranch, she had unknowingly touched on one of his hot buttons and he'd damned near gone off like a Roman candle in a Fourth of July fireworks display.

He was a psychologist specializing in human behavior. He had been schooled not only in how to be a patient and observant listener but also how to keep his emotions in check. The last thing a client wanted to see from his therapist during a session was a judgmental expression or outright shock when they revealed some of their darkest secrets. Those psychology tools had served him well over the years and he had used them quite successfully as a professional poker player to keep from alerting his opponents to the cards he had been dealt.

But when it came to Taylor, it was as if his skills didn't even exist. All she had to do was look at him with those big green eyes of hers and his training seemed to go right out the window.

The first time he'd noticed his uncharacteristic reaction to her had been when she told him that she wanted the other half of the ranch. She'd looked him square in the eye and the passion and determination in her striking green gaze had sent a streak of heat straight to the region south of his belt buckle. He had even found himself wondering if she would be that passionate when he made love to her.

His body tightened to an almost painful state and he rattled off every curse word he could think of. He forcefully slammed the car door and locked it with the remote. As he walked back to the house, he glanced down at the small bag in his hand. She couldn't have put much more than a few changes of clothes in it, indicating that she wouldn't be staying more than a night or two. That suited him just fine.

The sooner she went back to California and left him

alone, the better. Then maybe he could figure out what the hell had gotten into him and what he was going to do to get rid of it.

Well before dawn, Taylor rolled over in bed and glanced at the clock on the bedside table. She hadn't been able to sleep more than a couple of hours and those had been filled with fitful dreams of the tall, dark-haired man sleeping in the bedroom directly across the hall from hers.

Deciding she couldn't stand another minute of tossing and turning, she sighed heavily, threw back the covers and sat up on the side of the bed. How was she going to get Donaldson to sell her his interest in the ranch and leave the Lucky Ace for good? And why on earth did she find him so darned attractive?

She still wasn't entirely convinced that he hadn't somehow managed to cheat her grandfather in that poker game. But Donaldson had presented a compelling argument for his innocence and even though she knew how good her grandfather was at the game, she was starting to have her doubts. After all, he was human and as much as she hated to admit it, he could very well have made a mistake when he mentally calculated his odds of winning that fateful hand.

But what disturbed her the most about Donaldson was her reaction to him. The moment he'd approached her at the party to introduce himself, she had caught her breath, and she wasn't entirely certain she had breathed normally since. She had never experienced that kind of reaction to any of the men she'd dated in the past, let alone one she had just met and didn't trust.

Exhausted from the emotional roller coaster she had been on for the past three weeks and unsettled by her reaction to the man across the hall, she decided to do the one thing that always helped her put things in perspective. After a quick shower, she was going to start cooking.

Twenty minutes later, Taylor tied her damp hair back in a ponytail as she walked into the spacious kitchen. After washing her hands and starting the coffeemaker, she prepared to get to work. Checking the pantry and refrigerator for available ingredients, she decided on what she would make for breakfast then reached into one of the cabinets for a set of mixing bowls.

"Do you mind if I get myself a cup of coffee?" a deep male voice asked from close behind her.

Jumping, she almost dropped the bowls she held as she spun around to face Donaldson. Her heart racing, she took a deep breath. "I think you just took ten years off my life."

"Sorry," he said, hanging his hat on a peg by the door before pouring himself a mug of coffee. "I didn't mean to scare you. I thought you heard me." His deep chuckle sent a wave of goose bumps shimmering over her skin. "It's kind of hard not to make noise in a pair of boots on a hardwood floor."

Her heart skipped a beat as her gaze traveled the length of him, down to his scuffed cowboy boots. No man had a right to look that good so early in the morning.

Last night at the party, she had thought he was extremely handsome in his dark blue jeans, white oxford-cloth shirt and expensive caiman-leather boots. But that was nothing compared to the way he looked now. Wearing well-worn jeans and a chambray work shirt, he was downright devastating. With his dark eyes, black hair and a fashionable day's growth of beard stubble, Donaldson had that bad boy appeal about him that was sure to send shivers up the spine of any woman with a pulse.

Disgusted with herself and her wayward thoughts, Taylor set the metal mixing bowls on the counter and reached for a carton of eggs. "Where's my grandfather's housekeeper?"

"Marie retired right after the first of the year and I just haven't gotten around to hiring another one," he answered.

She wasn't surprised. The woman her grandfather had hired after her grandmother died had to be getting close to seventy. But on the other hand, she wouldn't have put it past Donaldson to have fired the woman, either.

"I'll have breakfast ready in a few minutes," she said, cracking eggs into one of the bowls with one hand while she reached for a whisk with the other. "Why don't you have a seat at the table?"

"What are you making?" he asked as he sat down at the head of the oak trestle table that had been in her grandmother's family for over three generations.

"Blueberry and ricotta–stuffed French toast with blueberry syrup, link sausage and blueberries and cantaloupe covered with vanilla sauce," she said, dipping extra thick slices of bread in the cinnamon-spiced egg mixture before placing them on the heated stovetop griddle.

"Sounds good, but isn't that a little fancy for a typical ranch breakfast?" he commented. "You must really like to cook."

She shrugged. "Since I graduated from the California School of Culinary Arts, then went to Paris for a year to study pastry, you might say I'm rather fond of it."

"Do you have your own restaurant?"

Arranging the food on two plates, she shook her head. "No, I'm a personal chef. I'm mainly hired for dinner parties and other special in-home occasions, like graduation and anniversary celebrations."

"That sounds like an interesting job," he said conversationally. "Do you have many clients?"

Nodding, she poured vanilla sauce over the fruit. "When I first started, I registered with the personal chef association and they referred clients to me. Now the majority of the calls I get are referrals from clients or from people who have attended the dinner parties I've prepared."

"You must be good at what you do," he said, sounding thoughtful.

Taylor carried the plates over to the table and sat down. "I'll let you be the judge." She watched him eye the food in front of him as if he wasn't sure it was safe to eat. Barely resisting the urge to laugh, she asked, "Is something wrong?"

"You made your opinion of me quite clear last night, so I'm sure you can understand my hesitation," he said, giving her a deliberate smile.

"It's true that I don't completely trust you, but that doesn't mean you can't trust *me*." She switched his plate with hers. "Now you have no reason not to try it."

Picking up his knife and fork, he cut into the French toast. "What do you say we start over?" he suggested. "The least we can do is be civil to each other until you go back to Los Angeles."

"I agree that being polite to each other would make negotiations for my buying your share of the ranch a lot easier," she agreed, taking a bite of fruit.

"I told you last night I'm not selling. But you could always sell your half to me," he said, taking a bite of toast.

"Absolutely not. I love the Lucky Ace. It represents the best part of my childhood." Irritated by his offer to buy her share, Taylor put her fork down to glare at him. "My grandfather knew how much this place meant to me and he intended for me to have it. I'm not selling it to you or anyone else."

Donaldson calmly took a sip of his coffee. "Then before you go back to Los Angeles, we'll have to work out an agreement on how I run the day-to-day operations and how often you want to receive dividend checks."

"I'm not going back to L.A.," she said, taking great satisfaction in the annoyed expression that came over his handsome face.

A forkful of toast halfway to his mouth, he slowly lowered it back to his plate. "What do you mean you aren't going back?"

Her appetite deserting her, she rose from the table to scrape the contents of her plate in the garbage disposal.

"I have every intention of making the Lucky Ace my permanent home."

"What about your clients back in Los Angeles?" he asked, looking more irritated with each passing second. "And that backpack wasn't big enough to hold more than a handful of clothes."

"I informed my clients of the move over a week ago and arranged for another chef to cover the dinner parties I had scheduled," she said, watching the frown lines on his forehead deepen further. "I sublet my apartment, stored my furniture, and the clothes I was unable to bring with me in the car, I shipped here. Those cartons should arrive sometime next week. I told you last night when you went out to get my backpack that I was here to run the ranch and would get the rest of my things from the car today."

He suddenly got up from the table, walked over to scrape his plate, then reached for the hat hanging beside the back door.

"Will you be back for lunch?" she asked.

"No."

"Then I'll have plenty of time to clean my room this morning before I bring my things in from the car and put them away this afternoon," she said thoughtfully.

"I'll go over to the bunkhouse and see if I can get one of the men to help you with that," he answered without turning around.

Before she could thank him for his thoughtfulness, he opened the door to walk out onto the porch then forcefully pulled it shut behind him.

"He took that better than what I thought he would,"

she murmured as she started rinsing their dishes to put into the dishwasher. She wasn't sure what she had expected, but Donaldson's passive acceptance of her moving into the ranch house hadn't been it.

Of course, she wasn't foolish enough to think that he had given up trying to get her to sell her part of the ranch to him. But maybe now that he knew she was serious about living at the ranch, he was giving a little more thought to selling her his.

Lane rode his blue roan gelding across the pasture toward the barn at a slow walk. He had to find some way to get Taylor to sell him her share of the ranch. Or if that wasn't something she was willing to do, at least get her to go back to Los Angeles and leave him the hell alone.

He could appreciate her sentimentality about the place her grandfather owned. But he had become attached to the property as well. For the first time in over twenty years he had a place he could truly call his own. It felt good and he wasn't willing to give that up.

As he stared off across the land, he thought about the plans he had for the future. He'd made a fortune playing poker and having invested wisely, he never had to work another day in his life if he didn't want to. But he didn't consider playing poker or ranching actual jobs. Poker was a pastime. He enjoyed the challenge of competing with other equally skilled players and if he ever lost interest in it, he'd quit with no regrets. But ranching was a lifestyle, and up until six months ago, he hadn't even realized how much he had missed it. That's why he intended to improve the Lucky Ace by introducing a herd of free-range cattle, as well as start raising and training roping horses for rodeo.

But all that could change if Taylor insisted on living on the ranch and taking an active role in running it. That's why he spent the entire day riding fence, repairing windmills and tightening gates, whether they needed it or not. Keeping busy helped him think. Unfortunately, he didn't arrive at any conclusions other than that Taylor was just as stubborn about selling her share of the ranch as he was.

When he'd won half of the Lucky Ace last fall, he had fully intended to sell it back to Ben. But the old man had asked that Lane move in and oversee the day-to-day running of the ranch while he spent the winter with his family in California. Ben had told him they would talk again in the spring and Lane could let him know if he still wanted to sell the property back to him. It had seemed like a reasonable request and Lane had agreed. But the past six months had reminded him of his time at the Last Chance Ranch and he'd decided that he might have been a little too hasty about offering to sell his interest back to Cunningham.

Lane stared off into the distance. As it turned out, being sent to the Last Chance Ranch as a teen and placed in the care of his foster father, Hank Calvert, had been the best thing that had ever happened to Lane and he had nothing but fond memories of the time he'd spent there.

Hank had been the wisest man Lane had ever had the privilege to know. He'd not only taught the boys in his care to work through their anger and self-destructive behavior by using ranch chores and rodeo, he had taught them a code of conduct that they all adhered to even as adults. Lane and the men he still called his brothers had all become honest, productive members of society because of their time with Hank. Along the way, they had bonded into a family that remained as strong, if not stronger, than any traditional family tied together by blood.

He drew in a deep breath. Even though he had overcome his past, gained a family he loved and, with Hank's help, managed to save enough money from his junior rodeo earnings to make restitution to the people he had conned or stolen from, Lane didn't particularly like being reminded of his youthful problems.

Of course, he hadn't had much of choice in what he'd done. But stealing was stealing and whether he'd had a good reason or not, being a con artist and a thief was still wrong.

That's why he'd had such a strong reaction when Taylor accused him of swindling her grandfather. She had unwittingly reminded him of what he had been and what he might have continued to be if he hadn't straightened up his act.

Riding into the ranch yard, he dismounted Blue and led the gelding into the barn. As he removed the horse's saddle and began brushing the animal's bluish-gray coat, Lane reviewed his options.

He supposed he could sell Taylor his half of the ranch, then look around for another property. But he rejected that idea immediately. Texas might be a huge state, but there weren't that many ranches the size of the

Lucky Ace up for sale. Nor were any of them located close enough that he would be able to see his brothers regularly or be there for them if they needed him. Besides, he had won his half of the ranch fair and square and no one was going to guilt him into selling it—not even a hot-as-hell redhead with the greenest eyes he'd ever seen and a figure that made him want to spend endless hours exploring it.

When his body stirred from just thinking about her, he stopped grooming the roan and cursed his neglected libido as he led the horse into its stall. That did it. When Lane started to find a woman who frustrated him to the brink of insanity attractive enough to incite a case of lust, it was time to do something about it. As soon as he took a quick shower and got ready, he was going to make a trip over to that little honky-tonk in Beaver Dam and see if he couldn't find a warm, willing female to help him scratch this itch. Maybe then he would be able to forget how desirable Taylor Scott was and start thinking of her as he would think of any other business partner.

With a firm plan in place, he walked purposefully across the ranch yard and climbed the porch steps. "Taylor, I won't be here for supper," he said as he entered the kitchen. "I'm going over to—" He stopped short when she vigorously shook her head. "What's wrong?" he asked, walking over to where she stood at the counter mixing something in a bowl.

She nodded toward the hall. "I can't get rid of the cowboy you assigned to help me carry my things in from the car," she whispered.

"I didn't assign him to do anything," Lane said, careful to keep his voice low. "When I mentioned you needed help, he volunteered."

"Whatever. I can't get him to leave," she insisted. "We finished unloading the car over an hour ago, but he keeps coming up with excuses to stick around. I even gave up putting my clothes away because I wasn't comfortable with him lurking in the doorway watching me."

Standing so close to her, breathing in the light scent of her herbal shampoo and noticing the perfection of her coral lips, caused every nerve in Lane's body to come to full alert. He took a step back, then another.

To distract himself from the temptation she posed, he asked, "Where's he now and what is he doing?"

"He's in the living room building a fire in the fireplace," she answered.

"It's May and the air conditioning is on. The last thing we need is to heat up the house with a fire," Lane said, frowning. "Whose bright idea was that?"

"Mine." She set the bowl aside and reached for some small white ceramic ramekins. "I had to think of something to keep him busy until you got back from wherever it was you went this morning."

"I was out riding fence and repairing some of the windmills," he answered defensively. He didn't owe her an explanation of his whereabouts, so why did he feel compelled to give her one?

"It's Sunday and after they tend to the livestock, even the hired men have the day off," she said, her tone disapproving. "Couldn't those chores have waited until tomorrow?"

It suddenly occurred to Lane that the impatience in Taylor's voice stemmed from her uneasiness about being around the man in the other room, not because she was annoyed by his daylong absence from the house.

"I'll get rid of him," he said, turning toward the hall. When he walked into the living room he found Roy Lee Wilks kneeling beside the fireplace, failing miserably at building a fire in the stone firebox. "Don't worry about the fire, Roy Lee. I don't think we'll be needing it. It's well over eighty degrees outside."

"Hey there, boss," the young man said, sitting back on his heels. "I wondered why Ms. Scott wanted me to build a fire." He removed his sweat-stained ball cap to run a hand through his shaggy blond hair. "I wasn't having much luck at getting it started anyway."

Lane checked his watch. "Marty should just about have supper ready over at the bunkhouse. It would probably be a good idea to get over there before Cletus eats his share and yours, too."

Putting his cap back on, Roy Lee rose to his feet and nodded. "I'll do that as soon as I check with Ms. Scott to see if she needs me to do anything else."

Lane shook his head. "Thanks, but you've spent most of your day off helping her and I'm sure you'd like to rest up before you move that herd of heifers over to the north pasture tomorrow morning. If she wants something else done, I'll take care of it."

The man looked as though he might want to argue the point, but apparently he decided that crossing the boss might not be a wise choice. "I guess I'll see you in the morning then," he finally said, turning toward the hall.

Lane leaned one shoulder against the kitchen doorway and waited for Roy Lee to bid Taylor a good evening and leave before he walked over to where she stood at the counter finishing the dessert she was working on. "Now that your problem is solved with Roy Lee, I'm going to take a shower and drive over to Beaver Dam for the evening."

"You won't be here for dinner?" she asked, looking disappointed. "I'm making prime rib, twice-baked potatoes with herbs and cheese, asparagus spears with hollandaise sauce and crème brûlée for dessert."

She had apparently been too distracted by wanting to get rid of Roy Lee to have heard him tell her earlier that he was leaving for the evening. He shifted from one foot to the other as he stared into her crystalline green eyes. She was going to a lot of trouble making dinner and if the look on her pretty face was any indication, she was going to be extremely disappointed if he didn't stick around to eat it. He decided right then and there that if he wanted to talk her into selling her share of the ranch to him, or at the very least convince her to go back to L.A., he was going to have to placate her. Otherwise, he wouldn't have a snowball's chance in hell of getting her to agree to anything.

"I thought you might not feel like making dinner after spending the day unpacking and arranging your things," he lied.

She gave him a smile that caused a hitch in his breathing. "Cooking is one of the ways I relax."

"Do I have time to take a quick shower before dinner?" he asked, unbuttoning the cuffs of his work shirt.

"Sure." She placed the ceramic ramekins in a pan with water in the bottom, then began to fill them with the crème brûlée mixture. "Everything should be ready by the time you come back downstairs."

Nodding, Lane clenched his jaw as he walked out of the kitchen and headed upstairs. He wasn't the least bit happy about the change in his plans for the evening. But there wasn't anything he could do about it now. It was one of those damned if he did and damned if he didn't situations where no matter what he chose to do, he'd be the one suffering the consequences.

Taylor would take it as a deliberate insult if he didn't have dinner with her and insulting her would make it impossible to talk to her about the future of the ranch. And then there was the matter of the itch he needed to scratch. Just being in the same room with her seemed to charge the atmosphere with a tension that sent hormones racing through his veins at the speed of light, reminding him that he was a man with a man's needs.

When his body tightened in response to that thought, he muttered a guttural curse and headed straight into the bathroom to turn on the cold water. Stripping off his dusty clothes, he stepped inside and hoped the icy spray would clear his head, as well as traumatize his body into submission.

As he stood there with his teeth chattering like a pair of cheap castanets, a plan began to take shape in his mind. If successful, it would settle things once and for all. And the sooner he got Taylor to agree to it, the better.

If he didn't, he had a feeling one of two things would happen. She would either drive him completely insane or he would end up suffering frostbite on parts of his body that no man ever wanted to think about freezing.

Three

"Thank you for getting rid of Roy Lee for me," Taylor said as she sat down in the chair Donaldson held for her. "I was so relieved to finally have him out of the house, I forgot to thank you earlier."

He shrugged as he sat down at the head of the table. "I don't think he meant any harm."

"Probably not," she admitted. "He's just always seemed a little creepy to me, even as a teenager."

"So you've known him a long time?"

She nodded. "He started working summers here before he got out of high school." Pausing, she had to think back. "That would have been about twelve years ago."

"Besides overstaying his welcome this afternoon, has Roy Lee ever said or done anything else that made you feel uncomfortable?" Donaldson asked, taking a sip of the cabernet she'd had him open and pour for them.

"Not really." Pushing the asparagus spears around her plate with her fork, she tried to put into words how she felt whenever she was around the man. "I know it's probably just my imagination, but he seems to watch every move I make." Looking up, she added, "You know, like those paintings with eyes that follow you around the room." She couldn't keep from shuddering. "He's that kind of creepy."

"I'll try to make sure he stays away from the house," Donaldson said, taking a bite of his prime rib. Swallowing the tender beef, he smiled. "This is really good."

"Thank you," she answered, hoping her cooking worked its magic and put him in a good mood. "I'm glad you like it."

They fell into an awkward silence for the rest of the meal and by the time they finished dessert, Taylor's nerves felt ready to snap. Yesterday she had tried talking him into selling his share of the ranch to her and that hadn't worked. Hopefully there was something to the old adage that the way to a man's heart was through his stomach. Only in this case, she was hoping to appeal to his sense of justice. The Lucky Ace had been in her family for years and her grandfather had known just how much the place meant to her. He'd always told her that one day he wanted it to be hers and not once had he mentioned that he intended for her to share it with someone else.

"After we get the kitchen cleaned up, I'd like to discuss something with you," Donaldson said, interrupting her troubled thoughts.

"About the ranch?" she asked, afraid to hope that he had changed his mind and was going to be reasonable about it.

He nodded as he rose to his feet and reached for her empty ramekin. "It's a nice evening. I thought we could go out on the front porch and watch the sun go down while we talk."

Getting up from the table, she walked over and began rinsing their dishes to put into the dishwasher while he put the leftover prime rib in a plastic storage container and placed it in the refrigerator. As they worked side by side to clean the kitchen, Taylor's nervousness increased tenfold, and it had nothing whatsoever to do with their upcoming discussion about the ranch.

Why did she have to notice how handsome Donaldson looked in his black shirt and jeans? And why did he have to smell so darned good? There was something about the combination of expensive leather and the scent of clean male skin that was just plain sexy.

Their fingers touched as he handed her their wineglasses and Taylor felt a streak of longing course straight through her. She came dangerously close to dropping one of the delicate crystal goblets.

"It won't take me more than a few minutes to finish up here." She cleared her throat and hoped her voice didn't sound as husky to him as it did to her. "Why don't you go on out to the porch?"

"Are you sure?" Was that relief she detected in his

deep baritone? Had he felt the tension surrounding them as well?

Forcing a smile, she nodded. "I won't be long."

When he turned and walked down the hall toward the front of the house, Taylor placed her forearms on the sink and sagged against it. How could one man exude so much sex appeal? And why on earth wasn't she impervious to it?

Lane Donaldson was the intruder—the enemy—and the very last man she should find appealing. But as she finished wiping off the counters, she had to admit that beyond his devastating good looks, there was a certain charm about him that any woman would find hard to resist. How many men still had the manners to hold a chair for a woman when she sat down at the table? Or insist on retrieving her bag from the car and carrying it upstairs, especially after she had accused him of stealing part of her grandfather's ranch?

She did feel a bit guilty about that. But at the time she had been angry and certain that her grandfather had been victimized by Donaldson. But now?

She still wasn't sure that he hadn't exploited her grandfather. But there was one thing she was certain of—he wasn't going to take advantage of her.

"All finished in the kitchen?" Donaldson asked over his shoulder when she pushed the screen door open and walked out onto the porch a few minutes later. He was sitting on the steps with his forearms propped on his knees, staring out at the sun sinking low in the western sky.

"There wasn't really much left to do," she answered, walking over to sit in the porch swing.

They were both silent for several long minutes before he finally spoke again. "I've been thinking about our situation," he said slowly. "And I'm pretty sure I've come up with a solution."

"Are you going to sell me your share of the ranch?" she asked. As far as she was concerned, that was the only acceptable answer.

His deep chuckle sent a shiver streaking up her spine. "No. And I'm betting you aren't willing to sell me yours."

"Not a chance," she shot back.

"I figured as much." He got to his feet and walked over to lean one shoulder against the porch support post in front of her. "But I think the one thing we do agree on is the fact that the way things are now is unacceptable."

She nodded. "You're right about that. There's nothing about this that I find even remotely acceptable."

"Before I tell you what I have in mind, I'd like to ask that you hear me out before you give me your answer," he said, folding his arms across his wide chest. "Do you think you can do that, Taylor?"

His deep baritone voice saying her name caused her to catch her breath. "A-all right. What have you come up with?"

"I want us to play poker," he said, meeting her questioning gaze. "If you win, I'll sell you my share of the Lucky Ace and you'll be rid of me for good."

Taylor's heart sank. Her grandfather might have been a world-class poker player, but she had never taken an interest in the game and didn't have a clue about how to play. What chance would she have against someone like Donaldson?

Besides, she wasn't entirely certain she could trust that he would play honestly. And even if he did, he was a professional and in the same elite category as her grandfather had been. She wouldn't have a prayer of winning against him.

"And if you should happen to win?" she asked, knowing she wasn't going to like his answer.

He smiled. "If I win, you go back to California and I stay right here."

"Absolutely not," she said, shaking her head. "I'm not taking a chance of losing my share—"

He held up his hand to stop her. "You promised to hear me out."

Glaring at him, she folded her arms beneath her breasts. "All right," she conceded. "Continue."

"I didn't mention anything about you losing your interest in the ranch," he said calmly. "If I win, you would retain your half of the place, go back to California and be content with occasional visits. And I'm sure we can come to an agreement on how often you want to receive reports and dividend checks, as well as sign documents stating that if either of us ever decide we want to sell our share, we'll give the other the first right of purchase."

Suspicious, she asked, "Why are you willing to be so generous? You told me that if I won, you would sell me your half. Doesn't that work both ways? Wouldn't you want my share if I lost?"

"It's true that I'd like to own the entire property,"

he admitted. "But I know this land belonged to your grandfather and that you have a sentimental attachment to it. I respect that and wouldn't ask you to give it up if it means that much to you."

"Why do you want it?" she demanded. There had to be a reason behind his stubbornness about not selling his part of the ranch and she was determined to find out what it was. "You don't have the same ties to it that I do."

He paused for a moment as he stared down at his boots. When he looked up, he shrugged his broad shoulders. "I finished growing up on a place a lot like this one and until I moved here last fall, I didn't realize how much I missed living on a ranch."

"Surely there are other places you could buy," she said, hoping he would see reason. "Texas isn't the only state with ranch property. I'm sure you could find something suitable somewhere else. And you wouldn't have a business partner. You would be the sole owner."

"All of my brothers have ranches that are close by or within a few hours' driving distance from here and there's nothing the size of the Lucky Ace for sale that isn't at least a day's drive away." He smiled. "I'm sure you can understand my wanting to be close to my family, as well as not wanting to settle for something that isn't what I really want."

Staring at him, she couldn't help but wonder what it was like to want to be close to family. Being the only child of a couple who should have never married, the only family member she had ever been close to was her grandfather. Spending all of her summers with him on the Lucky Ace until she enrolled in cooking school after high school graduation had been her only reprieve from her parents' constant arguing. That's why it meant so much to her. It represented the tranquility that she'd never had at home. But that wasn't something she felt comfortable sharing with just anyone, and especially not with Donaldson.

"So what do you think?" he asked when she remained silent. "Would our playing a game of cards for the ranch be a viable solution to our problem?"

"I'm going to have to give it a lot more thought before I decide," she said, wondering if there was a poker gene that she might have inherited from her grandfather. She knew there probably wasn't, but all things considered, it would have been nice if there had been.

He smiled. "Neither one of us is willing to go anywhere else, so there's plenty of time for you to make your decision."

"I think I can safely say I'll have an answer for you within the next day or so." Taylor rose from the swing and started toward the front door. Turning back, she started to add that she'd like the issue settled as soon as possible, but she forgot what she was about to say when she ran headlong into his broad chest.

He immediately wrapped his arms around her to keep her from falling. "Sorry. I didn't…expect you to switch directions."

As she stared up into his dark brown eyes, her breath lodged in her throat. She felt completely surrounded by him and the feeling wasn't at all unpleasant.

Her heart skipped several beats.

"I...um...I think I'll...turn in for the night," she stammered, unable to think clearly. What on earth was wrong with her?

He brought one of his hands up to brush a strand of hair that had escaped her ponytail from her cheek. The tips of his fingers lingered on her skin just a bit longer than was necessary and sent a tingling sensation pulsing through her.

When he lowered his head, she held her breath a moment as she awaited his kiss. But instead of covering her mouth, Lane's lips lightly brushed her ear as he whispered, "Sleep well, Taylor."

When he slowly released her and took a step back, it took a moment for her to realize he was looking at her expectantly. "Was there something else?" he asked.

"Um...good night...Lane," she finally managed.

Forcing herself to move, she opened the screen door and didn't stop until she was upstairs with her bedroom door shut firmly behind her. As she leaned back against it, she had to remind herself to breathe. Lane had more raw sensuality in his little finger than most men had in their entire bodies.

Her heart suddenly began to pound against her ribs. When had she started thinking of him by his first name? And why?

It had been much easier and a lot less personal to keep him compartmentalized as Donaldson, her adversary—the man she had suspected of cheating her grandfather. The very man who stood between her and her goal of owning all of the Lucky Ace.

Taylor scrunched her eyes shut as she tried to wipe

out the image of him holding her gaze as he leaned toward her. She had thought he was going to kiss her. And heaven help her, she hadn't made a single move to stop him.

"Get a grip on yourself," she muttered as she pushed away from the door. She wasn't interested in a one-night stand, a relationship or any other kind of entanglement with a man. She had watched her parents and the miserable existence that their marriage had become for the past twenty-eight years. And if there was one thing she had learned it was what she didn't want in life.

Grabbing her nightshirt, she headed into the adjoining bathroom. As she changed clothes and brushed her teeth, she tried to tell herself that she had been distracted by his proposal and hadn't been thinking clearly. But staring into the mirror, she shook her head at the woman staring back at her. She could try to justify her reaction all she wanted, but the fact of the matter was, she was attracted to him. And she wasn't the least bit happy about it.

Stepping out of the shower, Lane shivered and reached for a towel to wipe away the rivulets of cold water running down his body. Two cold showers in less than twelve hours was more than any man should have to endure, and he for damned sure had no intention of suffering through a third.

After Taylor ran into him on the porch and he had put his arms around her, he'd seen the anticipation in her emerald eyes. As a result, he had spent the entire night wide-awake and feeling as if he was going to climb the walls. Walking into the bedroom now, he quickly got dressed and pulled on his work boots. He was going downstairs and over breakfast, he was going to tell Taylor that he definitely wouldn't be home for dinner. If he didn't scratch this itch, there was a very good chance he would be a complete lunatic and a straitjacket away from being committed by the end of the week.

His only hope of any kind of reprieve from the situation would be for one of them to leave the Lucky Ace. That's why he had proposed a game of poker for control of the ranch. It had been the only thing he could think of that she might agree to.

If his instincts about her were correct, Taylor would want to win the Lucky Ace back by playing the same game Ben had lost. Lane was sure that in her mind it would vindicate her grandfather once and for all, as well as give her the satisfaction of beating him at his own game.

His conscience had reminded him that he was a professional and might have an unfair advantage. But surely Ben had taught Taylor his strategy and style of playing during her many visits to the ranch. If anything, that would make the game more interesting, and he hoped that she took him up on his offer to decide the fate of the ranch that way.

When he walked into the kitchen a few minutes later, instead of finding Taylor making breakfast, he found her talking on the phone. Who in the Sam Hill could she be carrying on a conversation with at five in the morning?

"He just came downstairs for breakfast," she said, smiling. "Would you like to tell him yourself?"

Lane frowned. "Who is it?"

"One of your brothers," she said, handing him the cordless phone.

As she turned toward the counter and whatever it was she was preparing for their meal, Lane cringed as he put the phone to his ear. The last time he'd received a phone call from one of his brothers this early in the morning, it was to tell him that his foster father had died from an undiagnosed heart problem.

"What's up?" he asked, walking down the hall to the study. He wasn't sure which one of his brothers was on the other end of the line, but it didn't matter. They were always there for each other and always would be.

"You're talking to the proud daddy of a healthy baby girl," Ryder said, sounding happier than Lane could ever remember.

Relieved that the news wasn't something bad, Lane grinned as he lowered himself into the desk chair. "Congratulations! How are Summer and the baby doing?"

"They're both doing just fine," Ryder answered. "Summer is understandably tired, but things couldn't have gone any better for either of them."

"That's great. And how are you holding up?" Lane asked, laughing.

"I face two thousand pounds of pissed-off beef on a regular basis without so much as blinking, but watching Summer go through labor was the most intense thing I've ever experienced," Ryder said, sounding as if he was glad everything was over with. "Let's just say I'm recovering and leave it at that."

"Glad to hear it. What's my new niece's name?" Lane asked, settling back in the chair.

"I'm leaving that up to Summer." Ryder paused as if a wave of emotion threatened. When he finally continued, his voice was extremely husky. "I don't care what she decides to name the baby. I swear I didn't think it was possible to fall in love with something so tiny so damned fast."

"You're going to be a great dad," Lane said, feeling his own chest tighten. Clearing his throat, he teased, "I can just see you now, sitting on a little chair with your knees threatening to bump your chin while you sip imaginary tea out of a tiny pink teacup."

Ryder laughed. "I'll be more than happy to do it. Whatever my little girl wants, my little girl gets."

"When do we all get to meet the newest member of the family?" Lane asked, hoping it would be soon. Since Sam and his wife had little Hank, he had really started to get into being a proud uncle.

"When I talked to Sam a few minutes ago, he said that Bria and Mariah have been planning a family dinner for the past couple of weeks in anticipation of Summer having the baby," Ryder answered.

"That doesn't surprise me," Lane said. "You know how much Bria loves family get-togethers. Just let me know when they're planning on having it and I'll be there."

"I sure will, bro," Ryder assured him. "Now, before I hang up and call the rest of the guys to tell them about the baby, would you like to let me in on who Taylor Scott is and what she's doing answering your phone at this time of morning?"

"It's a long story," Lane hedged, not all that eager to try explaining the situation.

"Why don't you give me the thumbnail version?" Ryder pressed.

Lane sighed heavily. He should have known better than to think he could end the call without his brother wanting to know what was going on. He'd do the same thing with any of his brothers if their roles were reversed.

"She's Ben Cunningham's granddaughter," Lane said, hoping that would satisfy Ryder's curiosity.

"Did she come back from California with Ben?" his brother asked.

"No, Ben passed away about three weeks ago." Lane ran his hand over the tension building at the back of his neck. He wasn't surprised that his brother wanted more of an explanation. If he was in Ryder's shoes, he would want details, too. "And before you ask when she arrived, Taylor is the redhead who crashed the party the other night. Ben left her his share of the ranch."

"I'm sorry to hear that about Ben. I know the two of you became pretty good friends after you won half of the Lucky Ace," Ryder said, his tone sympathetic. "But you don't sound all that thrilled about being in the ranching business with his granddaughter."

"We'd be just fine if she'd go back to California where she belongs and leave me alone," Lane admitted. "She's decided that she is going to take up residence here and actively run the ranch."

"Oh, this sounds like a story I've got to hear," Ryder said, sounding a little too happy about Lane's predicament.

"You're not going to let this go, are you?" Lane asked, already knowing the answer.

"Hey, Freud, you didn't let things go when I was being a stubborn jackass before I finally asked Summer to marry me," Ryder shot back.

Lane should have known that the intervention he and his brothers staged when Ryder had decided he wasn't good enough for Summer would come back to bite him in the butt. "There are absolutely no similarities between the situations," Lane said, shaking his head at his brother's erroneous comparison. "You were head over heels in love. I'm not." He snorted. "Hell, I'm not even sure if I like her. She's stubborn, opinionated and about as prickly as a cactus patch."

"In other words, she's a challenge and that makes her all the more attractive to you, doesn't it?" Ryder asked knowingly.

Lane gritted his teeth. "Have I told you lately what a smart-ass you can be?"

"No. But whether you wanted to or not, you just answered my question," Ryder said, sounding quite smug.

If he could have reached into the phone and got hold of his brother, Lane would have cheerfully throttled him. "Goodbye, Ryder."

"Later, bro."

Ryder's laughter echoed in Lane's ear long after he

ended the phone call. He loved all of his brothers, but sometimes they irritated the life out of him. Ryder was reading way more into his partnership with Taylor than was there. And before the sun cleared the eastern horizon, the rest of his brothers would know all about it.

Lane groaned. There wasn't a doubt in his mind that along with announcing the birth of his daughter, Ryder was already spreading the word that Lane was living under the same roof with Taylor. And once his brothers put their spins on the facts, the next time they all got together, Lane's life would be a living hell from all of their good-natured ribbing.

But they'd have it all wrong. Any attraction he felt for Taylor had more to do with his long dry spell of being without the warmth of a woman than anything else. She was beautiful and had a smoking-hot body. He was a healthy adult male who had neglected his basic needs. And they were stuck in a house together because they were both too stubborn to give on the issue of who was going to live on the ranch. It just stood to reason that until he released some of his built-up tension he was going to find her desirable.

Confident that his perspective had been restored, he rose to his feet and walked straight to the kitchen. "Taylor, I won't be home for dinner this evening. I have to make a trip over to Beaver Dam."

Lane parked his truck next to Taylor's little red sports car, switched off the lights and muttered a word he reserved for the direst of situations. His trip to the Broken Spoke over in Beaver Dam had turned out to be a huge waste of time. And it wasn't because there weren't any interested women present. There was one cute little brunette in particular who'd made it crystal clear she was available for an evening of no-strings-attached fun. But he hadn't even been able to work up enough enthusiasm to ask her to dance.

What the hell was wrong with him? He still felt edgy enough to jump out of his own skin. The woman had been more than willing and he'd made the hour's drive over to the watering hole specifically for just such an encounter.

But as he got out the truck and slowly walked up the porch steps, he decided that he wasn't going to do any kind of self-analysis in an effort to understand his reaction to the situation. He had a feeling that he wouldn't be overly happy with what he discovered about himself if he did.

"I didn't expect you back this soon," Taylor said when he entered the kitchen. Sitting at the kitchen table, she had a laptop set up in front of her. She quickly closed it as if there was something on it that she didn't want him to see. "Would you like a cup of coffee?" she asked.

"Why not?" he muttered. It wasn't as if the caffeine would prevent him from sleeping. The woman staring at him had taken care of that ever since her arrival. When she started to get up, he shook his head. "I'll get it."

"I've been thinking," she said as he poured his coffee, then walked over to sit down at the head of the table.

He wasn't sure he wanted to know, but taking a sip from the mug in his hand, he asked, "About?"

"Your suggestion that we play cards for the Lucky Ace," she answered.

She caught her lower lip between her teeth as if she was still trying to make up her mind. It was all Lane could do to keep from groaning. He'd like nothing more than to do a little nibbling of his own on her perfect coral lips.

The thought caused his heart to stall. Where had all this desire to kiss a woman been when the brunette at the Broken Spoke had flirted with him? With sudden clarity, he knew exactly what the problem had been. The woman at the Broken Spoke hadn't been a redhead with the greenest eyes he'd ever seen.

He came dangerously close to repeating the word he'd muttered when he parked his truck and prepared to enter the house.

"If I agree to your terms, I would definitely want an impartial observer to witness the game and verify the outcome," she said, oblivious to his turmoil.

"Absolutely," he said, thankful that she had distracted him from his sudden realization. "With the stakes this high, I wouldn't have it any other way."

"Where would the game be held?" she asked. "Here or somewhere neutral?"

"Since gambling is illegal in the state of Texas, we'd have to go over into Louisiana," he said, shaking his head. When he won, he wanted to make sure that everything was aboveboard and there was no question about the validity of the game.

"Why not go to Las Vegas?" she asked, looking a bit suspicious.

He shrugged. "It's fine with me if that's where you want to go. I just figured it might be easier to go to Shreveport, since it's just a few hours away and won't involve extensive travel arrangements."

She frowned. "I hadn't thought about it being so much closer. That probably would make it the obvious choice."

"I have a friend who owns one of the finest casinos over there." Confident now that she was going to agree to his plan, he smiled. "I could talk to him about setting up a private room for us, with our own dealer, of course."

"Is that where you played my grandfather when you won part of the ranch?" she asked suddenly.

He didn't like her tone or the suspicion in her green gaze. "Yes."

"Then I'd rather not play there," she said, shaking her head.

"Why not?" he demanded. He had a good idea what she was driving at and he didn't like it one damned bit.

"Nothing against the man, but I'm sure you can understand that I'd feel more comfortable with someone who wasn't one of your friends taking care of the arrangements," she said determinedly as she got up to get herself more coffee.

Lane set his mug on the table with a thump and rose to face her. "Let me set you straight on something right now, babe. Cole Sullivan is one of the most honest men I've ever known. He's not only a trusted friend of mine, he was a good friend of your grandfather's, as well."

When she took a step back, he took a step forward. "In fact, Ben knew Cole for years before I met him."

"Oh, I didn't realize…I, uh, just want to make sure the game isn't compromised…" Her voice trailed off as she once again began to worry her lower lip.

"In other words, you want to make sure that I don't cheat," he said, advancing on her.

"I didn't…say that," she stammered, backing up until her retreat was stopped by the kitchen cabinets.

Bracing his hands on the countertop on either side of her, he leaned forward to make his point, effectively trapping her. "I know it's hard for you to believe, but I didn't cheat your grandfather and I have no intention of cheating you." As he stared down at her, the anger in his gut evolved into heat of another kind. Lowering his tone to a more intimate level, he reached up to trace her jawline lightly with his index finger. "Believe me, Taylor, if it isn't going to be a clean, honest game, I won't play."

He noticed the same anticipation in her eyes that had been there the evening before. This time, Lane couldn't have stopped himself if his life depended on it.

"I'm going to do what I should have done last night." Holding her gaze with his, he slowly began to lower his head.

"W-what…is that?" she asked, sounding delightfully breathless.

"I'm going to kiss you," he said, covering her mouth with his.

Four

Lane's lips molded to hers and Taylor couldn't work up so much as a token protest. The truth was, she had wanted him to kiss her the night before and been disappointed when he hadn't. Her reaction was totally insane, considering that she still wasn't entirely sure she could trust him, not to mention that it was completely out of character for her. But there was no denying that she felt a level of attraction to him that she'd never felt for any other man. And it appeared there wasn't anything she could do to keep from giving in to it.

But when Lane closed his arms around her and drew her close, she abandoned all contemplation of her atypical behavior. Teasing her lips with his, he sought entry to deepen the kiss, and his soft exploration, the gentleness of his tongue stroking hers, caused a delightful little quiver deep in the pit of her belly. When she placed her hands on his broad chest, the strength she detected in the hard contours beneath his shirt reminded her of the contrasts between a man and woman and set her pulse to racing. What would it be like to feel those muscles pressed to her much softer body as he made love to her?

The thought stunned her out of her daze. Why was she fantasizing about Lane Donaldson? He was the man who stood between her and having what she wanted—the entire ranch. Quickly she pushed against his chest.

"I…uh, that…shouldn't have—" Why couldn't she get her mind and vocal cords to work in unison?

Instead of releasing her, Lane continued to hold her against him. "I'm not going to apologize for something we both wanted," he said, shaking his head.

"I didn't want…I mean, I suppose I was curious, but—" She clamped her lips together and rested her head against his chest in defeat when it was apparent that her thoughts were still too scattered to be coherent.

His low chuckle vibrated against her ear, sending warmth spreading throughout her body. "Now who's being less than honest?"

Not trusting that she wouldn't make a bigger fool of herself than she already had, she simply shrugged.

"So are we agreed that I'll call Cole Sullivan tomorrow and have him set up the game for us?" he asked.

"I'm not sure what to do." How was she going to play a card game with the stakes so high when she had no idea what she was doing?

Placing his finger under her chin, he tipped her head

up until their gazes met. "What aren't you sure of, Taylor? Me? The integrity of the game we'll play? What?"

As she stared up into his dark brown eyes, she sighed heavily. "I'm not sure I'll be able to play with you or anyone else," she finally said, shaking her head.

He frowned. "Why not?"

His gentle tone was playing havoc with her senses and before she could stop herself, she blurted out, "I don't know the first thing about poker."

"You've never played?" he asked, looking as if he couldn't quite believe it. "Didn't Ben at least teach you the basics?"

She shook her head. "I know it sounds bizarre, considering that he was a legendary player and considering how much time I spent here, but I was more interested in doing other things with him, like going horseback riding or fishing down at the creek."

"Then playing for the Lucky Ace is out of the question," he said slowly.

"Yes, we are going to play, eventually. While you were away this evening, I've been doing some research online and it doesn't look like the game of poker would be all that difficult to learn. I'm just unsure of how long it will take me to master it," she said, walking over to the table to open her laptop. "I'm not missing my only chance to get your half of the ranch."

It irritated her no end when Lane threw back his head and laughed out loud. "You've got to be kidding."

Snapping the laptop shut, she turned to glare at him. "I couldn't be more serious."

"Poker isn't something you learn overnight," he said,

grinning, as he shook his head. "Besides the fact that there are several different card games referred to as poker, you also need to learn the rank of the different hands, when to stay and when to fold, how to bet and how to read the other players. And that's just the tip of the iceberg, babe."

"Are you so arrogant you think there's too much for a woman to learn?" she asked, her anger increasing with each passing second.

"Not at all." His easy expression was replaced by a dark scowl, indicating that he took her accusation as an insult. "Some of the best and most challenging players I know are women. So don't accuse me of thinking women aren't intelligent enough to learn the game, because that's not the case."

"Then what *are* you trying to say?" she asked.

"I'm trying to tell you that it isn't as easy as just learning the fundamentals of the game." He picked up his coffee cup from the table and walked over to empty it in the sink. "A website or a book can't teach you how to recognize a player's tell or how to conceal your own. And don't think that's something you can learn by reading something online. It takes practice, patience and learning to be extremely observant of the other players."

Taylor nibbled her lower lip. She had no idea what he was talking about. What was a tell? But she wasn't going to let her lack of knowledge deter her. Even if one of the poker websites couldn't furnish her with a definition and show her how to recognize it, she was certain if given enough time she could figure it out.

"We don't have to play the game tomorrow," she said,

wondering how long it would take her to find a website explaining the skills he'd outlined and then how much longer it would take to become good enough to beat him.

He smiled. "If you want to go back to California and take the time to learn how to play, we can always set up things when you think you're ready."

"What do you hear when I tell you something?" she demanded, propping her hands on her hips.

His frown deepened. "What do you mean?"

"Either my voice comes out at a decibel you can't hear or you have a serious listening problem," she stated flatly. "I told you that I'm not going back to California, unless of course the outcome of the game goes in your favor. Then I'll hold up my end of the bargain and move. But only then." Her confidence restored, she smiled. "You might as well accept it, Lane. I'll be staying right here until we play that game."

She could tell by the muscle working along his lean jaw that he wasn't the least bit happy. But that was just too darned bad. She had every right to stay at the ranch and nothing he could say would convince her to do otherwise.

Deciding that she needed to do more research, she picked up her laptop and started toward the hall. But a sudden thought had her turning back. "You said there are several card games that fall into the poker category. Which one will we be playing?"

"Texas Hold'em," he answered tightly.

She nodded. "Then that's the one I'll concentrate on learning. And at some point before the game, I'll draw up a document with the details of our agreement. We'll both sign it and have it witnessed by an outside party."

His lips flattened into a line. "You still don't trust me, do you?"

"At this point, I'm not sure whether I do or not. But I've always heard it's smart to get things of this nature in writing," she said, turning to go upstairs. "Let's just call it insurance against either of us changing our minds about the game we'll be playing or against a misunderstanding of what we get if we win."

As she went upstairs to her room, she hoped there really was some kind of skill or natural talent for playing poker that she might have inherited from her grandfather. It would make everything so much easier. She could not only learn the game quickly, she might be able to hold her own playing cards with Lane and quite possibly beat the socks off of him.

She couldn't help smiling at the thought. Nothing would please her more than to beat Lane at his favorite game. She would not only make the Lucky Ace whole again, but she would be avenging her grandfather's lapse in judgment for betting the ranch in the first place.

As she plugged in her laptop and sat down on the bed, Taylor nibbled on her lower lip. All things considered, she probably should have turned Lane down and requested they do something else to determine who would control the ranch. But she hadn't been willing to take the chance that he would withdraw his offer completely. And the last thing she wanted was for him to own any part of the ranch for an extended period of time.

Besides, she was intelligent and learned things quickly. It was perfectly reasonable for her to believe she had a fighting chance at winning.

When Lane went upstairs for what he knew for certain would be another sleepless night, he glanced at the closed bedroom door across the hall. He could see a narrow strip of light reflected on the hardwood floor beneath it and he'd bet every dime he had that Taylor was visiting websites, researching how to play Texas Hold'em.

If he had known that she'd never played before, he wouldn't have suggested a poker game to decide the fate of the ranch. But when he'd given her the opportunity to call it off, she'd refused.

He released a frustrated breath. The woman was too stubborn for her own good. There was no way it could be a fair game. Not when he was a professional and she had no idea what she was doing. So what was he supposed to do?

Trying to go the fair and honorable route hadn't worked, and his conscience wouldn't allow him to take advantage of her inexperience. But it appeared elephants would start roosting in trees before she backed down. The way he saw it, there was only one thing he could do that might come close to solving the problem.

Shaking his head at the ridiculousness of the entire situation, he stepped across the hall and knocked on Taylor's door. He couldn't believe what he was about to do, but there wasn't any other choice.

"Is something wrong?" she asked when she opened her door.

She looked absolutely adorable in her lime-green midlength gym shorts and a hot pink T-shirt with butterflies screen printed across the front. On any other woman he wouldn't have found the outfit all that appealing, but Taylor somehow managed to make it look sexy. Real sexy.

His mouth went as dry as a Texas drought when he realized she wasn't wearing a bra. "No, nothing's wrong," he finally managed as he shifted his weight from one foot to the other in an effort to relieve the pressure beginning to build behind the fly of his jeans. "I've been thinking that if you insist on playing cards for the ranch, you're going to need someone to give you a crash course on how to play."

"The only person I knew who could play well enough to teach me how to beat you at cards was my grandfather," she said, shrugging one slender shoulder.

He nodded. "And since that's no longer possible, I see no other alternative but to teach you myself."

Her eyes widened and he could tell she was thoroughly shocked by his offer. "Excuse me?"

"It's the only option that makes sense," he insisted, wondering if she had finally driven him over the edge. Even he was finding the idea absurd. "We both know you can learn all you need to know about the rules of the game and the ranking of the hands from a website. But it can't teach you what to expect when you're facing me across the table in a live game."

"Do you think I've lost my mind?" she asked, laughing. "Why would you want to help me learn to play a game that I fully intend to win? And what guarantee would I have that you'd be honest about what you teach me? For all I know, you might teach me something that will ensure that you come out on top."

"First and foremost, your grandfather was a good friend. I'm making the offer to help you because of the admiration and respect I had for him. And secondly, contrary to what you think of me, I have a conscience and a set of ethics I live by." For reasons he didn't quite understand himself, he was determined to set her straight about his morals once and for all. "When we play for the ranch, I want it to be a fair game and one that we both have a chance of winning. Otherwise, you might as well pack your bags and head back to L.A. now."

She raised an eyebrow. "Oh, so you think you're that good, huh?"

He grinned. "I know I am, babe. That's why I'm willing to help you out."

When she started to nibble on her lower lip, he reached out and placed his finger to her mouth, stopping her. "Lesson number one. Stop worrying your lower lip when you're trying to decide what to do. That's one of your tells and lets me know that you're unsure."

"I have more than one?" she asked.

Staring down into her expressive green eyes, he nodded. "When you think you have the advantage, you smile." He cupped her face with his hands. "And when you think I'm going to kiss you, your eyes widen slightly in anticipation." He slowly began to lower his head. "Just like they're doing right now."

As he covered her mouth with his, Lane knew he was flirting with disaster. They were rivals for the Lucky Ace and she could very easily accuse him of trying to use their attraction to convince her to sell him her share. Or worse yet, she might think he was trying to win her trust only to betray it later when he taught her how to play poker.

He didn't like either prospect, but there didn't seem to be anything he could do to stop himself. Every time he got within arm's length of her, all he could think about was kissing her the way she was meant to be kissed—and a whole lot more.

Tracing her lips with his tongue, Lane coaxed her to open for him. When she sighed softly and allowed him entry, he didn't think twice about deepening the kiss to stroke her inner recesses. Never in all of his thirty-four years had he tasted anything as erotic or sensual as Taylor's sweetness. When she circled his neck with her arms and leaned into him, he pulled her more fully against him and the feel of her lithe body pressed to his had him harder than a chunk of granite in less than the blink of an eye.

His heart stalled and a surge of heat shot straight through him when a tiny moan escaped her parted lips as she sagged against him. He had expected her to pull out of his arms and give him hell for his reaction, but to his immense satisfaction, it appeared that she was as turned on as he was. With sudden clarity, Lane realized that the tension between them had just as much to do with an undeniable chemistry drawing them to-gether as it did their rivalry over who would own all of the Lucky Ace.

The discovery wasn't something he was at all com-fortable with. Needing time and distance to think, he eased away from the kiss and took a step back. "I should probably let you get some sleep," he said, knowing he was facing another cold shower and another night of feeling as if he could climb the walls.

Staring down at her, he couldn't help but notice the blush of desire on her creamy cheeks and the slightly dazed look in her emerald eyes. He knew beyond a shadow of doubt that she would be as passionate about making love as she was about getting his share of the ranch.

The thought sent a surge of heat knifing through him and he quickly turned to cross the hall to his bedroom. "We'll get started on you learning the fundamentals of the game after breakfast in the morning."

"I haven't agreed to let you teach me how to play," she reminded him.

With his hand on the doorknob, he turned back. "If you have a better idea, I'd like to hear it."

"I...well, no," she admitted.

"Do you think you can win on your own without me teaching you?" he asked, knowing full well she couldn't.

She started to nibble on her lower lip, then stopped herself and shook her head. "I suppose it wouldn't hurt for you to show me a few things about the game." She paused for a moment and then shrugged, adding, "If that's what you want to do."

He almost laughed out loud. If he hadn't realized before how fiercely independent she was, he did now. She had to make it sound as if she would be doing him a favor to let him teach her how to play so she could beat him. Normally, that attitude would irritate the hell out of him. But coming from Taylor, he just found it cute and…endearing?

Quickly opening the door to his room before he crossed the hall and took her back into his arms, he grinned. "Pleasant dreams, Taylor. I'll see you in the morning."

The following morning, Taylor yawned as she finished loading and starting the dishwasher. She had spent most of the night visiting websites and researching all she could on the game of Texas Hold'em. At least, that was the excuse she was going to use if Lane asked her why she was so sleepy. She wasn't about to admit to him or anyone else that after that kiss at her bedroom door last night, she couldn't have slept if her life depended on it.

Both times Lane had kissed her, she'd felt as if she would melt into a puddle at his big booted feet. And neither time had she been able to work up the slightest resistance. All Lane had to do was start lowering his head and every ounce of sense she possessed seemed to desert her. Never in her entire life had a man had such a drugging effect on her.

A shiver slid up her spine when she closed her eyes and thought about how his lips felt as they explored hers. He wasn't aggressive the way some men were.

Lane's firm lips softly moved over hers with such care—it was as if he worshipped her. Her lips tingled from just the memory of it.

Taylor opened her eyes and shook her head. She needed to get her mind off Lane and his addictive kisses. Her full attention needed to be focused on what she had learned about the card game they would be playing. His lips on hers might be the most erotic thing she'd ever experienced, but he was still her rival and she had every intention of beating him at his own game in order to regain all of the Lucky Ace.

Forcing herself to concentrate on the information she'd read on the internet, she still wasn't sure about the ranking on a couple of hands, but for the most part it seemed pretty straightforward and fairly easy. They would each be dealt two cards facedown, known as their "hold," then three community cards called the "flop" would be dealt faceup. They would be given the opportunity to bet, then the next card, called the "turn," would be dealt faceup and they would be given the chance to make another wager. When the last card, called the "river," was dealt, they would once again bet and the object was to make the best five-card hand out of their hold cards and the five community cards face up on the table.

Now all she had to do was let Lane teach her when and how much to bet on the different hands and what to look for when she was trying to discover someone's tell.

Yawning again, she poured herself a cup of coffee and walked over to sit at the kitchen table to wait for her first poker lesson. Lane had gone to the barn right after he helped her clear the table to have Judd, the ranch foreman, call the farrier to come to the ranch to put new horseshoes on the working stock. He should be back soon, and she wanted to be ready.

Taylor nibbled on her lower lip before she could stop herself. It appeared he knew more about ranching than she had first thought. He'd mentioned that his brothers had ranches in the area and that he had finished growing up on one. Did that mean they had all lived in a town or city before moving to a ranch?

"What's running through that overactive mind of yours now?" Lane asked, walking over to the table.

Lost in thought, she hadn't even realized he'd entered the house. "You mentioned that you finished growing up on a ranch," she said, choosing her words carefully. "Was it around here?"

He shook his head as he sat down beside her. "It was up close to Dallas—about eight miles southeast of Mesquite."

"I've been to the rodeo up there," she said, remembering the times she and her grandfather had made the two-hour trip for the weekly summer events.

Lane smiled. "I used to compete in that rodeo every weekend when I was home on summer break."

"Really?" The more she learned about him, the more she was finding Lane to be one surprise after another. She would never have guessed he'd been a rodeo contestant.

Nodding, he reached for the deck of cards lying on the table in front of them. "My foster brother T.J. and I competed in the team roping event until he decided to concentrate on the bareback bronc riding."

It suddenly occurred to her why he had mentioned that he finished growing up on a ranch. Lane had been a child of the foster care system.

"And before you ask, yes, I was a foster care kid," he said, as if reading her mind. He peeled the cellophane wrapper from the new deck of cards and took them out of the box. "I was sent to the Last Chance Ranch when I was fifteen—right after my mom passed away from breast cancer."

"I'm sorry, Lane." She reached over to place her hand on his forearm. "That's such a young age to lose your mother. But what about your father? Couldn't you have lived with him?"

The only outward sign that she might have touched a nerve was the muscle working along his lean jaw. "He died a couple of years before my mom."

"Didn't you have any other family you could have lived with?" she asked. Even though her mother and father's parenting had been far from stellar, Taylor couldn't imagine not having anyone.

"No, both sets of my grandparents were dead. My dad did have a brother in the military, but he got killed in the Middle East. And my mom was an only child." He shrugged as he began to shuffle the cards. "But it all worked out. When I went to live on the Last Chance Ranch, I gained five brothers and a father that anyone would be proud to call family, and I consider myself one of the luckiest men alive to have them."

"So you still stay in touch with your foster father as well as your brothers?" she asked.

He shook his head. "Hank Calvert died several years ago. Much like your grandfather, he had a heart problem that he chose to ignore instead of getting the medical treatment he needed."

They were silent for a moment before she frowned. "But how did you know I was curious about your being a foster child?" she asked. Was the man psychic?

He reached over to trace her lower lip lightly with his index finger. "Remember what I told you last night about worrying your lip when you're unsure or trying to decide something?"

"My tell," she murmured.

His gaze held hers as he slowly nodded. "I could see you were curious about my brothers, but that you couldn't decide if you should ask about them." He smiled. "What about you? Ben mentioned he had family in California, but he didn't say if you had siblings."

"I used to think it would be nice to have a brother or sister." She shook her head. "Then the older I got, I decided it was just as well that I was an only child. I wouldn't wish my childhood on anyone."

Lane put the cards down. "Why do you say that?" His eyes narrowed and his voice held a hard edge when he demanded, "Were your parents abusive?"

"No. Not at all." Taylor took a sip of her coffee. She didn't like to talk about her parents, but since Lane had shared details about his upbringing, she felt it was only fair to share hers. "My mother and father are the most mismatched couple you'd ever care to meet and they should have never married. They have nothing in common, lead separate lives and when they are together, they argue constantly." She sighed. "The only peace I ever had as a child was the summers I spent here on the Lucky Ace with my grandfather."

"Did they ever talk about getting a divorce?" he asked, his tone gentle.

She nodded. "They've hurled that word at each other on a daily basis for as long as I can remember. But neither one of them ever intend to carry through with it."

Lane frowned. "Was it because of not wanting you to come from a broken home?"

"No, it was something much simpler than that," she answered. "In fact, I don't think my becoming a child of divorce even crossed their minds."

"How could it not?" he asked, frowning.

"They were too busy trying to figure out a way to get around the state divorce laws." She smiled at his skeptical expression. "California is a community property state and they would have had to divide everything equally. Neither of them wanted the other to get any part of their assets. They both wanted it all."

"I'm sure they would both have wanted you," Lane said, sounding more sure of that fact than she was.

"Maybe if they had ever come to an agreement about the bank accounts and property, they might have discussed it," she said, rising from her chair to refill her coffee. Taking a mug from the cupboard, she poured Lane a cup of the steaming brew as well, then set it in front of him. "But I've often wondered if they would have argued as passionately about who got custody of me as they did over the money and the house—if they'd ever gotten that far along in the discussion."

When she sat down, he reached over to cover her hand with his. "I'm sure you were their most important consideration, Taylor. I know it didn't seem that way at the time, but I'm betting that you never doubted that they loved you."

She shook her head. "No, that was never an issue. I always knew they both loved me very much."

"And they're still together?" he asked. "Even now that you're grown and have a place of your own?"

"Yes." She shrugged. "I assume it's because whoever outlives the other wins and gets everything."

"That could be," he admitted, lightly touching her cheek with his knuckles. "But it might be that's just the type of relationship they have. They bicker a lot, but deep down they love each other. I'm not saying that's definitely the case with your parents, but there is that chance."

"I suppose it's a possibility," she admitted, stopping herself just before she started nibbling on her lower lip.

Lane's slow grin caused her pulse to race. "Now, I'm going to move to the opposite side of the table."

Confused, she frowned. "Why? Aren't you supposed to be showing me how to play?"

"That's why I'm moving across the table from you." His deep chuckle as he moved to the chair opposite her caused warmth to spread throughout her body. "If I don't put a little distance between us, I'm going to be tempted to take you in my arms and kiss you until a poker lesson is the last thing on either of our minds."

Five

Two hours after he moved to the other side of the table, Lane sat back in his chair and smiled at the woman seated across from him. "I don't know about you, but I'm ready for a break," he said, rotating his shoulders. "It's a nice day. What would you say about going for a horseback ride?"

"Actually, that sounds pretty good," she said, smiling. "It's getting close to lunchtime. I could pack some sandwiches and we could find a nice shady spot for a picnic down by the creek."

"While you get those ready, I'll go saddle the horses," he said, rising to his feet. "Was there a particular horse you rode when you were here to visit Ben?"

She nodded. "The buckskin mare is mine. Grandpa

gave her to me for my sixteenth birthday." Looking uncertain, she asked, "Has anyone been riding her?"

"I think Judd told me someone tries to ride her at least once a week," he said, referring to the ranch foreman. "Why?"

"Horses that haven't been ridden in a while can get ornery," she said, smiling. "I just wanted to know what to expect."

Lane grinned as he grabbed his hat from the peg beside the door and put it on. "Not in the mood for a rodeo, huh?"

Her laughter sent a shaft of heat straight through him. "I haven't ridden in several years and I'm going to be sore enough as it is. I'd rather not end up with a broken bone or two on top of that."

"There's a set of insulated saddlebags in the pantry and there should be a couple of ice packs in the freezer," he said, reaching for the doorknob. "When you get everything ready, call the barn and I'll bring the horses up to the house."

"Why?" she asked, opening the refrigerator.

"The saddlebags are going to be heavy and I don't want you to have to carry them," he said, quickly stepping out onto the back porch before he grabbed her and kissed her until they were both numb from lack of oxygen.

He muttered a curse and walked across the ranch yard toward the barn. The entire time he had been teaching her which poker hands to keep and which ones to fold, all he'd been able to think about was how much he wanted to do a whole lot more than just kiss her.

He shook his head at his own foolishness. What in hell was wrong with him? He'd gone over to Beaver Dam to get some much needed female attention and quickly discovered that none of the women appealed to him. Yet all he could think about was Taylor and the attention he'd like for them to give each other.

"Hey there, boss," Roy Lee greeted him when Lane entered the barn. "Judd told me to tell you that he called the farrier and he'll be here tomorrow to put new shoes on the working stock."

Lane nodded as he walked down the barn aisle toward the man. "Thanks for letting me know. Where's Judd now?"

Roy Lee took off his cowboy hat to wipe the sweat from his brow. "He took Cletus with him to check out the grazing conditions in the north pasture."

"What did you do to piss Judd off?" Lane asked, eyeing the wheelbarrow and pitchfork Roy Lee was using to muck out the stalls.

"Oh, I'm not in hot water," he said, shaking his head. "I volunteered to clean out the stalls."

"Why?" Lane asked, frowning. If there was anything a cowboy hated more than just about any other ranch chore it had to be mucking out stalls.

"Somebody had to do it," Roy Lee said, shrugging. "And Cletus was complaining that he'd cleaned the stalls for the last three days. I just thought I'd give him a break."

Lane had a good idea why the cowboy was being so accommodating and it had nothing whatsoever to do with giving the other hired hand a break. "Blue will be gone for a while, so you'll have plenty of time to get this one done," he said as he opened the half door, snapped the lead rope onto the gelding's halter, then led him out of the stall.

"Going for a ride?" Roy Lee asked, sounding a little too curious.

"We'll be gone until sometime this afternoon," Lane said, nodding.

"I'll hang around close," Roy Lee offered, his tone almost giddy. "You know, in case Ms. Scott needs help with anything."

The man had just confirmed Lane's suspicions. He was hanging around close to the house on the off chance he would get the chance to talk to Taylor.

"That won't be necessary," Lane said, tying Blue to a grooming post.

He started back toward the buckskin mare's stall when Roy Lee insisted, "I don't mind at all, boss." He laughed. "You know how women are. They're always changing things. She might decide she needs to rearrange furniture and wants me to move some of the heavier stuff for her."

"Not today," Lane said, leading the mare to the hitching post to be saddled along with his roan. "She's going to be with me."

Roy Lee's cheerful expression quickly changed to one of disappointment. "Well, I guess I'll get back to work then, boss."

Lane almost felt sorry for the poor guy as he slowly walked back to the stall he'd been cleaning. It was clear the man had a huge crush on Taylor and had hoped to spend some time with her. But Roy Lee had no way of knowing that he made Taylor extremely uncomfortable by staring at her.

Of course, Lane had to admit that the young cowboy wasn't the only one who couldn't take his eyes off Taylor. Several times while they'd been playing cards, Lane had caught himself gazing at her, and not just to observe her tells. He'd noticed how her copper-colored hair framed her heart-shaped face and complimented her peaches-and-cream complexion. And he'd never seen eyes so green or filled with so much expression. He could tell exactly what she was thinking just by looking into their emerald depths and he couldn't help but wonder how they would look filled with passion as he made love to her. His body twitched and his jeans suddenly became a little too tight in the stride.

Not at all happy with the direction his thoughts had taken, he yanked the cinch tight on Blue, causing the roan to grunt. "Sorry, buddy," he muttered, patting the gelding's bluish-gray coat.

Quickly saddling the mare, Lane untied the reins of both horses and led them out of the barn. He'd do well to stop daydreaming about his business partner and focus on teaching her to play poker. The sooner they played that game and the fate of the Lucky Ace was decided, the better off he would be. Otherwise he was going to be in a perpetual state of arousal and completely out of his mind in very short order.

A sudden thought caused him to slow his steps. His and Taylor's situation was not unlike her parents' and their selfish refusal to share their assets. Wasn't that what he and Taylor were doing with the Lucky Ace? They were both too stubborn to give in, sell their interest in the ranch and move on to find something else.

But he rejected that train of thought immediately. He and Taylor weren't tied together by the bonds of marriage or in any other way, except for joint ownership of the property. They both had their reasons for wanting to hang onto it and none of those reasons had anything to do with an egotistical game of one-upmanship.

By the time Lane reached the house, he decided not to give it any more thought. He needed a break and fully intended to relax and enjoy the rest of the day without thinking about which one of them would end up controlling the ranch.

When he tied the horses to a hitching post by the steps, he crossed the porch and went inside. "Are you ready to go?"

Taylor was nowhere in sight, but he could hear her voice as she came down the hall. "That sounds very nice," she said, walking into the kitchen with the phone. When she saw him, she mouthed, "It's one of your brothers."

Lane immediately shook his head. The last thing he wanted to do was listen to whichever one of them was on the other end of the line rib him about living under the same roof with a hot-as-hell redhead.

"Okay, I'll be sure to tell him," Taylor said, ending the call. Smiling, she placed the cordless unit on the charger. "That was your brother Sam. He said to tell you that the dinner they're having to welcome the new baby is a week from Sunday at Ryder and Summer's place."

"Sounds good." Lane smiled. "We can ride over there together." He didn't have to ask if she would like to go with him. He knew his brother well enough to know Sam had already issued the invitation.

"I don't know," she said, sounding uncertain. "Sam asked me to join the celebration, but I don't want to intrude on your family gathering."

Lane shook his head. "It wouldn't be an intrusion at all." He stepped forward and without giving it a second thought, took her into his arms. "I can guarantee you'll enjoy yourself, especially getting to know the three women."

He barely stopped a groan from escaping when he watched her nibble on her lower lip for a moment before she finally nodded. "All right. I'll think about it."

Taking a step back, he decided that it would be in both of their best interests for them to start that horseback ride sooner rather than later. "Are you ready to go?"

"Absolutely," she said, giving him a smile that sent his blood pressure soaring.

Lane picked up the packed saddlebags from the kitchen island and followed her out of the house. As he watched her put her foot in the stirrup and swing up into the mare's saddle, his heart stalled and the pressure in his jeans increased. The sight of her slender legs straddling the mare had him wondering what it would feel like to have them wrapped around him as he sank himself deep inside of her.

Mentally running through every curse word he'd ever heard, he tied the bags to the back of his saddle and mounted the roan. He immediately had to shift to a more comfortable position or risk emasculating himself.

What was it that Taylor had that other women didn't? Why was she more attractive to him than any other woman he'd ever known? And what in the name of all that was holy could he do to stop it?

As a trained psychologist, he had the tools to fight what he suspected was a growing addiction to her. But as a man looking at a desirable woman, that same knowledge was proving to be completely useless.

"I can tell I haven't been on a horse in a while," Taylor said when they stopped at the creek and dismounted. Her thigh muscles and backside were sore, but riding her mare again was well worth a little discomfort. "I'm just glad Cinnamon has such a smooth gait."

"Otherwise you'd be sitting on a pillow for the next few days?" Lane guessed.

Laughing, she nodded as she waited for him to untie the saddlebags from the back of his horse. "A nice, hot soaking bath tonight should help."

"Some liniment probably wouldn't hurt," he said, carrying the saddlebags to a spot beneath a grove of cottonwood trees along the bank.

She reached for the blanket she had tucked inside one of the compartments to spread it out on the grass. "I wasn't sure what sandwiches you prefer, so I made a couple of different kinds."

"I'm pretty easy to get along with," he said, smiling. "I'm sure whatever you've made will be just fine. Besides, there hasn't been anything you've fixed yet that wasn't absolutely delicious."

His compliment pleased her more than she would have thought. "I'm glad you've gotten over your reticence about my cooking."

"Yeah, I owe you an apology for that." He grinned as he knelt beside her to help unpack their lunch. "But you were pretty clear that you wanted me off the ranch one way or another. As angry as you were the night before, I wasn't sure you hadn't decided to tamper with my food."

"I suppose I owe *you* an apology for that," she admitted. "I was tired and angry and might have overreacted just a bit."

"More like a lot, babe," he said, unwrapping a ham-and-cheese sandwich.

"I did make some pretty serious accusations, didn't I?" She wasn't proud of it, but her temper had gotten the better of her that night. "I'm sorry for bringing your integrity into question, Lane. But I just couldn't understand why Grandpa would jeopardize any part of the ranch. I still don't. It just doesn't make sense to me."

He put down his sandwich and wrapped his arms around her, pulling her to his broad chest. "Don't beat yourself up, Taylor. I got over it and after I cooled down, I realized that you'd had a tough few weeks. You'd just lost Ben, learned that he had lost part of the ranch you expected to inherit, then had to fulfill his last wish and bring his ashes back here." He ran his hands along her back in a soothing manner. "That kind of emotional roller coaster would put anyone on edge."

If Lane hadn't been so understanding, she might have

been able to stop herself. But his insight into what she had gone through with the loss of her beloved grandfather was more than she could bear. For the first time since her grandfather's passing, Taylor felt tears flow freely down her cheeks.

She hated to cry and had managed to hold the grief at bay until now. But once she acknowledged it, there was no way to stop it. Lane held her close as she sobbed against his chest and when the emotion finally subsided, he wiped away the last traces of her tears with one of the napkins she'd packed for their lunch.

Embarrassed by her uncharacteristic display, she stared down at her tightly clenched fists. "I'm so… sorry. I didn't…mean to do…that."

Placing his index finger under her chin, he lifted her gaze to meet his. "Don't ever be sorry for mourning someone you love, Taylor. It's part of the healing process. Was that the first time you've cried since you lost Ben?"

She nodded. "I don't like…being weak."

"Shedding tears for your grandfather's passing doesn't make you weak," he said gently. "It shows the strength of your love for him. And you should never apologize for loving someone that much."

His tender tone and the understanding she detected in his dark brown eyes caused a warmth like nothing she'd ever known to spread through her. With no thought to the consequences, Taylor pressed her lips to his.

She'd never in her entire life been the one to initiate a kiss, but Lane didn't seem to mind her assertiveness. Pulling her more fully against him, he took control and lightly teased her with nibbling kisses that were both thrilling and frustrating. She wanted him to deepen the caress, to kiss her like he'd done before.

Apparently sensing what she wanted, he coaxed her to open for him and her heart skipped a beat. At the first touch of his tongue to hers, stars burst behind her closed eyes and a streak of longing coursed through her.

As he softly stroked her inner recesses, he slid his hand under the tail of her T-shirt and the feel of his callused palm against her smooth skin sent ribbons of desire twining to the most feminine part of her. But when his hand covered her breast and his thumb grazed her nipple through her thin bra, a shiver of anticipation coursed through her and left her feeling weak with longing. The sensation was so strong it frightened her with its intensity.

"It's okay, babe," Lane said, apparently sensing her panic. He moved his hand from beneath her shirt, then, straightening the garment, added, "Nothing is going to happen that you don't want to happen."

That's what bothered her. She did want something to happen. She wasn't comfortable with it and she certainly wasn't about to tell him about it.

"I think it would be a good idea...if we stopped doing that," she said, sounding anything but convincing as she put some space between them on the picnic blanket. "We're rivals."

"Yeah, it's probably not wise," he said, his tone as unenthusiastic as hers. The slow, sexy grin curving the corners of his mouth made her feel warm all over. "But there's nothing wrong with a little *friendly* rivalry."

"Your kisses are way too sensual to be considered friendly." As soon as the words were out of her mouth, she wished she could call them back. She hadn't intended to let him know how his kiss affected her.

"What do you say we stop playing games and be honest with each other?" he asked, taking her by surprise. "We're both fighting an attraction that neither of us is comfortable with, but that both of us seem powerless to stop."

As she stared at him, she started to deny there was any kind of chemistry between them, but she couldn't. There was no sense lying about something they both knew to be the truth.

"Is that your professional opinion?" she asked, picking up one of the soft drinks.

"Just an observation," he said, shrugging.

They sat in silence as they finished their sandwiches before curiosity got the better of her. "So what do you propose we do about this so-called attraction?" she asked, wondering if she'd lost her mind. The smart thing to do would have been to change the subject and ignore his comment.

"I've given it some thought and the way I see it, we've got two options," he said, capturing her gaze with his. "We can either continue to let things go the way they've been going and be frustrated beyond reason, or we can explore this thing between us and see where it goes." His smile took her breath away. "It's my opinion that we should choose the latter."

"You've got to be kidding," she said, laughing. Surely he couldn't be serious.

"Think about it, Taylor." He gathered their empty sandwich wrappers and stuffed them into the saddlebags. "Trying to pretend it doesn't exist hasn't worked."

She couldn't argue with him on that point. It had been the elephant in the room, so to speak, practically from the moment they'd met. But she had studiously avoided a romantic entanglement with any man for so long, it was difficult for her to consider doing anything else.

"Are you saying you think we should start dating?" she asked, wondering if that's all he was suggesting.

He stared at her for several long moments as if trying to discern what she was thinking. "Are you interested in more?" he finally asked.

"No!" She hadn't meant for her answer to come out quite so forcefully. "I mean, I'm just not interested in a relationship."

"I'm not, either." He raised one black eyebrow. "I know what my reasons are. Would you care to share yours?"

"You know about my parents and the constant turmoil they're in. I would think it would be obvious," she stated flatly. "If that's what being part of a couple is, I'd rather not bother." She frowned. "Now it's your turn. Why are you resistant to the idea?"

He remained silent until they had the last traces of their lunch packed away in the saddlebags. "Playing poker is all about taking chances and accepting that sometimes you're up financially and sometimes you're down. I don't have that particular worry, nor will it ever be an issue for me because of the investments I've made.

I have the freedom to do whatever I want, when I want, without having to worry. But most women want stability, not a man who plays a game just for the fun of it," he said, getting up from the blanket. He held his hand out to help her to her feet. "I haven't met a woman yet who tempted me enough to consider giving that up."

"Did you always want to be a gambler?" she asked, folding the picnic blanket.

He shook his head. "I have a master's degree in psychology and had every intention of working in that field. But while I was in college there always seemed to be a poker game going on somewhere in the dorm and I'd join in after I got out of class for the day." He smiled. "After I won everybody's spare change, I figured out I was pretty good at it. Then my roommate suggested that I enter a tournament over in Shreveport." He tied the bags on the back of his gelding's saddle. "I did and the rest, as they say, is history."

As she mounted the mare, she thought about what Lane had told her. Why had she been disappointed when he mentioned that he'd never met a woman who'd made him think about giving up being a professional gambler? She certainly didn't want him to be tempted by her, did she?

"So what do you want to do?" he asked as they rode away from the creek.

Distracted with her disturbing thoughts, she asked, "About what?"

"Are we going to continue on as things are?" He smiled. "You know my take on the situation. I'd like to know yours."

"I'll give it some thought and let you know," she said evasively. She had never been one to make hasty decisions and she wasn't about to start now.

Six

Hurrying down the hall toward the front of the house, Taylor hoped whoever was knocking on the door turned out to be the delivery service with the things she'd shipped to herself from California. But her smile faded when she found Roy Lee standing on the porch.

"Sorry to bother you, Ms. Scott," he said, smiling. "But I was on my way back from a trip to the feed store and I thought I'd check to see if you need me to help you with anything today."

"No, but thank you for asking, Roy Lee," she said, wondering why he wasn't doing whatever work the foreman had assigned him for the day.

"Okay," he said, looking disappointed. He stood staring at her as if waiting for her to issue an invitation to come inside the house.

"Was there anything else, Roy Lee?" she asked, wishing the cowboy would just leave. She didn't want to be rude, but he was making her extremely uncomfortable.

"No. I just wanted to make sure you know I'm available if you need me." He continued to look at her for several long moments before he finally added, "I guess I'll let you get back to whatever you were doing." He started down the steps, then suddenly turned back. "If you do find something you need help with, just call the barn. I'll be more than glad to come back and take care of it for you."

"I'll remember that," she said, watching him walk to the ranch truck he'd parked next to the house.

Closing the door, she felt a chill slide through her. On impulse, she reached down to secure the lock. She wasn't sure what it was about the man, but she didn't trust him.

"Who was that?" Lane asked, coming out of the office.

"Roy Lee," she answered. "He wanted to know if I needed his help with anything today."

Walking over to her, Lane put his arms around her waist. "You know what his problem is, don't you?"

She shook her head as she tried to ignore the warmth that spread from the top of her head all the way to her toes from his touch. "If you have any kind of insight into what he's up to, please enlighten me."

"Roy Lee has a huge crush on you and unless I miss my guess, he's had it since you were teenagers," he said, smiling.

"That's ridiculous," she insisted. "I haven't been here for a visit in several years and besides, I've never given him the slightest bit of encouragement."

Lane grinned. "Let me clue you in on the way this works, babe. When a man finds a woman attractive, he's a lot like a banty rooster strutting around the hen house. He'll do whatever he thinks will get her to notice him. For Roy Lee, it's offering to help you out. He's trying to prove to you that he's handy to have around and that you need him."

"The only thing he's accomplishing is giving me a major case of the creeps," she said, shuddering. "I can't put my finger on what it is about him, but I'm just not comfortable being around him."

Pulling her to him, Lane hugged her close. "I'd be the last person to tell you not to trust your instincts, Taylor. But he's done nothing that would warrant me firing him."

"I'm not saying he should be fired." She rested her head against Lane's broad shoulder. "I just don't want to be around him."

"You don't have to be." He kissed the top of her head. "I'll be here to run interference while I help you practice your poker skills. And as added insurance that he doesn't bother you, I'll have Judd assign him to chores on another part of the ranch."

Feeling a little better about the situation, she tilted her head back to kiss his lean jaw. "Thank you."

"That's completely unacceptable," he said, smiling as he lowered his head. "If you're going to kiss me, I want the real deal."

As his mouth came down on hers, Taylor immediately melted against him. In the past couple of days she'd thought a lot about his suggestion that they acknowledge the magnetic pull between them, but she still wasn't sure what to do. Lane didn't want a relationship any more than she did, but a casual liaison had never been her style.

Unfortunately, it didn't seem that she had a lot of choice in the matter. Every time she was close to Lane, she forgot all the reasons she didn't want to get involved with him or any other man. All she could do was think about the way he made her feel.

When he traced her lips with his tongue and coaxed her to open for him, she gave up on trying to understand why she couldn't resist him and lost herself to the myriad sensations flowing through her. Her blood pulsed through her veins and an empty ache began to pool in her lower belly when he moved his hand to cup her breast. Even through her clothing, his touch had the magical effect of making her feel as if he truly cherished her. But when she felt his hard arousal pressed to her, she had to cling to him for support.

"Have you come to any conclusions on what we should do about this?" he asked, easing away from the kiss.

Gazing up at his handsome face, she shook her head. She would like nothing more than to throw caution to the wind and live for the moment. But that wasn't who she was and she wasn't about to pretend otherwise.

"I don't want you to think that I'm pressuring you, Taylor," he said, tucking a strand of hair that had escaped her ponytail behind her ear. "Nothing is going to happen unless that's what you want. But I'm not going to hide the fact that I want you, either."

They gazed at each other for several long moments before the ringing of the phone intruded. "I'll get that in the office," Lane said, kissing her forehead before he released her to go answer the call.

As she walked back into the kitchen, Taylor nibbled on her lower lip. There wasn't a doubt in her mind that it was just a matter of time before they both reached the limit of their frustration and gave in to the chemistry between them. A thrilling hum vibrated through every part of her at the thought.

Taylor sighed as she removed a roast from the refrigerator and began to cut it into cubes for the beef bourguignon she'd planned to make for their dinner. She only hoped when the moment came that she could keep things in perspective and not let her emotions get the better of her. Otherwise she had a feeling there was a very real chance she could get her heart broken.

After another one of Taylor's delicious dinners, Lane sat at the table watching Taylor glance at the five cards face up on the table between them, then at the two cards she was holding. For the first time since he'd started teaching her how to play, she wasn't giving her hand away with her tells. He couldn't help but be proud of her. She had caught on to the game quickly and her skills were progressing nicely. It wouldn't be too much longer and they would be playing for the ranch. So why did that thought leave him with a keen sense of dread? That was what he wanted, wasn't it?

The sole purpose of him teaching her to play poker was so they could engage in a game for control of the ranch. A game he had every intention of winning. But the thought of Taylor leaving the Lucky Ace to go back to California didn't hold nearly as much appeal as it had a week and a half ago.

"I'm *all in*," she said as she shoved all of her chips to one end of the community cards.

She was betting everything she had on the single hand and the odds were he had her beat. He had a full house, while the best she could hope for was a straight. He fleetingly thought about folding the hand and letting her win, but he'd never thrown a game in his life and she wouldn't want him to do that now. She was determined to win on her own and he admired that. Besides, she needed to learn to consider all the possible hands he could be holding and place her bet accordingly.

Counting out the equivalent number of chips, he added them to the pot. "I call."

He watched her take a deep breath as she turned over her two hold cards. "I have a jack-high straight," she said proudly.

"Very nice hand," he said, smiling. When she started to pull the pile of chips to her side of the table, he shook his head. "Unfortunately, it's not quite good enough." He flipped over his hold cards. "I have a full house. Jacks full of nines."

"Well, drat!" She frowned. "I really thought I had you that time."

He nodded. "You had a good solid hand and a damned good chance of winning. But you also needed to consider that with two jacks on the table, I could be holding a jack and that the other community cards would give me the full house."

"Which was exactly what happened," she said with a sigh.

"Hey, don't feel bad." Standing up, he walked around the table to pull her from her chair and into his arms. "If I'd had the straight, I would have had to consider going all in, too."

She tilted her head slightly. "But you wouldn't have, would you?"

"It depends." He kissed the tip of her nose. "In a tournament with other professional players, there are more cards in play and the odds are better that one of them would have the full house. But with just the two of us, the odds were in your favor of winning with the straight."

"So I didn't make a bad play?" she asked, snuggling against him.

With her delightful body aligned with his, he was finding it hard to draw his next breath, let alone think about playing poker. "No," he finally managed.

"When do you think I'll be ready to play you for the ranch?" she asked, leaning back to look up at him.

"I'd say within the next week or so," he answered evasively. He had a feeling that either way the game went, he would come out feeling as though he'd lost. But he didn't want to think about settling who would live on the ranch. With her in his arms, he had more pleasurable things on his mind. "Why don't we take a break and go out onto the front porch to watch the sun go down?"

"I think I'd like that," she said, giving him a smile that sent his blood pressure up a good ten points.

Ten minutes later, as they sat in the porch swing watching the last traces of daylight fade into the pearl-gray of dusk, Lane held Taylor to his side. They were both silent for some time and he couldn't get over how right it felt to be enjoying something so simple with her.

"Could I ask you something, Lane?" The sound of her soft voice saying his name caused heat to gather in his loins.

"Sure." Turning slightly to face her, he smiled. "What would you like to know?"

"Why did you go ahead and become a psychologist when you had already started playing poker profession-ally?" she asked.

He stared at her a moment before he answered. She had been truthful with him about her situation at home and her parents' constant turmoil, which he knew wasn't easy for her. He supposed it was only fair to tell her why he had chosen to study psychology.

"I wish I could tell you my reasons were noble and that I had wanted to help people. But I can't," he said, shaking his head. "I went into the field for one purely selfish reason. I was looking for answers."

"May I ask what you were questioning?" she said cautiously.

He didn't think about his biological father all that much anymore. After he'd been sent to live on the Last

Chance Ranch, Hank Calvert had become his dad and had been more of a parent to him than his real father ever had. Ken Donaldson had been too busy wining and dining clients in order to climb the corporate ladder in the world of high finance to be a good husband and father.

"I told you that my father died a couple of years before my mother," he said, choosing his words carefully. When she nodded, he went on. "What I didn't say was that he died by his own hand."

"Oh, Lane, I had no idea," she said, hugging him. "That must have been horrible for you and your mother."

He did his best to swallow the anger that always accompanied thinking about his father's death. "I went into psychology because I wanted to understand what he might have been thinking and how he could cause his family that kind of devastation."

She laid her soft hand on top of his. "Did you find the answers you were looking for?"

"Not really." Shrugging, he twined their fingers. "It would have been easier to accept if it had been something he couldn't help, like an undiagnosed chemical imbalance or some other psychosis that impaired his reasoning. But it wasn't."

"Did he leave an explanation why he thought death was his only answer?" she asked.

Lane clenched his jaw until his teeth hurt as he nodded. "My father selfishly took his own life because he was a coward." Unable to sit still, he released her and stood up to walk over to the porch rail. Gripping the board so tightly he wouldn't have been surprised if he'd left dents in the wood, he kept his back to her as he finished. "The note was with him when I came home from school and found him hanging from one of the rafters in the garage."

"Oh, my God, Lane! That must have been so awful for you," she said, her tone quavering.

"It was a sight that I'll never forget, as long as I live," he admitted. He took a deep breath. "He explained in the note that he was facing legal issues over some bad financial decisions and couldn't bear the loss of his reputation and financial ruin because of it." He paused a moment before he could force words past the resentment that choked him. "It was all about him and his pride. He didn't consider what it would do to my mother and me. Either that, or he just didn't give a damn about all of the emotional pain taking his own life would put us through."

"I'm so sorry, Lane," Taylor said, placing her hand on his back. Wrapped up in his anger, he hadn't even heard her get up from the swing. "I didn't mean to bring up something so painful for you."

Turning, he took her in his arms and held her to him like a lifeline. "It's all right. You had no way of knowing," he said, closing his eyes as he tried to wipe away the last traces of the memory. "It's been over twenty years and it's not something I allow myself to think about all that often. As far as I'm concerned, it's in the past, where it needs to stay."

When she framed his face with her palms and raised up on tiptoe to kiss him, his heart slammed against his rib cage. The kiss was brief and one of comfort more than anything else, but a need stronger than anything he'd ever experienced shot through him.

Lane couldn't have stopped himself if he'd tried as he pulled her more fully against him to deepen the caress. Heat streaked straight to the region south of his belt buckle as he explored her and reacquainted himself with her sweetness. He might not have known her for all that long, but he sensed that Taylor could very easily become his anchor—the one person who would renew his strength and help keep him grounded.

At any other time, the thought would have scared the hell out of him and would have sent him running as hard and fast as he could go in the opposite direction. But all he could think of, all he wanted, was to forget the ugliness of his past and lose himself in the beauty he knew he would find in her arms.

Her soft moan when he moved his hand to her breast and the way she pressed herself into his touch caused his heart to race and his body to harden so fast it left him feeling light-headed. He'd never been as aroused as he was at that moment and he knew he was going to go out of his mind if they didn't make love soon.

Easing away from the kiss, he took one deep breath after another in an effort to relieve some of the tension gripping him. "I think I'll go…for a walk," he finally managed.

"W-why?" Taylor's eyes were bright with desire, and the passion coloring her creamy cheeks was almost his undoing. Nothing would please him more than to see her look like that as he sank himself deep inside of her.

"I need you, Taylor," he said roughly. "And if I don't walk away now, I'm not going to be able to."

Instead of telling him to take a long hike off a short pier as he expected her to, she gazed up at him for several long seconds before she whispered, "I want you, too, Lane. I know it's probably not wise. But I do."

When Lane pulled her to him, shivers of anticipation coursed through her. Taylor wasn't about to think of the consequences of making love with Lane. He wanted her, and at the moment, she needed him more than she needed her next breath.

"Are you sure, Taylor?" he asked, kissing the side of her neck. "I don't want you feeling pressured. I'd rather go for a jog and take a cold shower than have you regret making love with me."

"The only thing I'll regret is if we don't make love," she said truthfully.

She watched him close his eyes and take a deep breath then, taking her by the hand, he led her into the house. Neither said a word as they climbed the stairs and walked down the hall toward their rooms. She wasn't at all surprised when he opened the door to his bedroom and stood back for her to enter. Very few men were comfortable amid ruffles and lace and besides, from everything she'd heard when she and her friends talked about relationships, men had a thing about taking women to their beds.

Looking around, she realized that her first impression of Lane had been correct. He was not only a Texan from the top of his Resistol all the way to his big leather boots, he was a cowboy through and through. He had painted the walls a soothing sage that complimented the Native American artwork and printed drapes perfectly.

As she continued to peruse the room, her gaze landed on the rustic king-size bed and her heart skipped a beat. The natural shades of red in the cedar logs were in sharp contrast to the black satin pillows and comforter. His choice of bedding wasn't what she expected, considering the rest of the decor. But as she stared at the bedding, she had to admit that the sheer sexiness of it suited the man she was about to make love with.

When he slipped his arms around her waist from behind, she leaned back against him. "It's all right if you're having second thoughts," he said, nuzzling the side of her neck. "I don't want you doing anything you aren't comfortable with."

Turning in his arms, she shook her head. "I'm not having second thoughts," she said, wondering if what she was about to tell him would have him changing his mind. "I'm not on any kind of birth control."

"Don't worry, babe. I'll take care of everything," he said, kissing the side of her neck.

Shivering from the delightful feeling of his mouth on her sensitive skin, she nibbled on her lower lip. "There's something else."

"What?" He sounded distracted as he bent down to remove her tennis shoes and his boots.

"I've…never done this before."

He went completely still a moment before he straightened to face her. "You're a virgin." It wasn't a question. He looked as if the concept was completely foreign to him.

"Yes. I believe that's what a woman is called when she's never had sex," she said defensively.

He looked doubtful. "You're twenty-eight."

"Yes, I am, and you're thirty-four." She frowned. "So what's your point?"

"I just thought you would have met someone you wanted to be with before now," he said, gently touching her cheek.

"I didn't say I haven't been tempted a few times," she admitted. "I just never felt I was with the right guy."

"And you think I'm the right man?" he asked huskily as he lightly ran his index finger along her jaw.

Taylor nodded. She couldn't explain it, but making love with Lane just felt right.

"If I take your virginity, it's not something I can give back, babe," he warned, capturing her gaze with his.

"I—I...know." The look in his dark brown eyes and the intimate deepening of his voice made it hard to catch her breath.

She watched him close his eyes a moment before taking a deep breath. When he opened his eyes, he stared down at her. "I should send you across the hall to your room."

"But you aren't going to do that, are you?" she asked, her heart thumping so hard against her ribs, she thought it might burst.

Lane slowly shook his head. "I'd like to do the right thing, but I want you too damned much to be gallant about this." He lowered his head to give her a kiss so tender it brought tears to her eyes. "Are you really sure this is what you want, Taylor? If not, say so now."

Reaching up, she took her hair down from her pony-tail. "There are a lot of things I'm not sure of, but right now making love with you isn't one of them."

When she tugged her tank top from the waistband of her jeans and started to take it off, he smiled and caught her hands in his. "I can take things from here."

Normally, she was very independent and wanted to do things for herself. But whether it was the situation or the man, allowing Lane to take the lead felt completely natural.

"I want you to tell me if anything we do makes you uncomfortable or if you change your mind," he said as he slowly lifted her top over her head.

Instead of reaching for the front clasp of her bra as she thought he would, he unsnapped the front of his chambray shirt and tossed it on top of her turquoise tank top. The sight of his well-developed chest and abdominal muscles sent a wave of goose bumps shimmering over her skin. Lane's body was absolutely beautiful.

Unable to stop herself, she ran her fingers along the ridges and valleys of his smooth skin. "You don't work out, do you?"

He shook his head as he allowed her to explore the well-defined sinew. "Any exercise I get is either from ranch work or shuffling cards," he said, his low chuckle seeming to vibrate all the way to her soul.

Fascinated by the contours of his upper body, it took a moment for her to realize that he had unhooked her bra. He parted it and slid the straps over her shoulders and down her arms. "You're absolutely beautiful, Taylor."

Cupping her breasts with his palms, his tender touch

sent a wave of heat flowing through her and she closed her eyes as she savored the erotic feeling. "I...that... what you're doing. It feels...amazing," she said, suddenly extremely short of breath.

"It's only going to get better, babe," he whispered as he lowered his head to take one of her nipples into his mouth.

The feel of his tongue circling and teasing her while his thumb gently chafed the other tight tip caused her body to pulse with a need stronger than anything she'd ever experienced. When he lifted his head to pay homage to her other breast, Taylor's heart sped up and her knees felt as if they were made of rubber.

Unsure how much longer her legs would support her, she placed her hands on his chest to brace herself. The feel of his warm masculine skin and his heart beating in time with her own sent a delicious heat coursing through her.

"Are you doing okay?" he asked as he reached for the button at the top of her jeans.

"I—I...think so," she answered, wondering if she would ever breathe normally again.

His appreciative smile as he eased the zipper of her jeans down made her feel as if she was the most cherished woman on earth. "Tell me what you're feeling."

"Warm and—" She paused as she searched for the right word to describe how she felt. "—restless. And my knees feel weak."

Instead of taking her jeans and panties off, he surprised her when he stepped back to unbuckle his belt. As she watched him unfasten his jeans, then slide them and his boxer briefs down his long, muscular legs, she realized he was taking the rest of his clothes off first in order to make her feel a bit more comfortable. An unfamiliar tightness spread through her chest at his thoughtful consideration.

When he kicked the rest of the garments toward the growing pile of their clothing, her heart stopped then took off beating double time. His body wasn't merely beautiful, it was magnificent.

As she appreciated his taut physique, her gaze traveled from his impossibly wide shoulders down his washboard abdomen and beyond. But her heart stalled and her eyes widened at the sight of his arousal and the heaviness below. Although she didn't have any experience and couldn't make an accurate comparison, she sensed that Lane wasn't a small man.

Her concern must have been apparent, because he closed the distance between them. He took her into his arms, kissing her tenderly. "We'll fit together just fine, babe."

Most of the time, she took exception to men calling her anything but her name. She felt it was insincere and condescending. When Lane used the endearment, though, it was genuine and made her feel as if she was truly special to him.

But she abandoned all speculation when he ran his hands along her sides, then beneath the waistbands of her jeans and panties. Capturing her eyes with his, he slowly caressed her hips and thighs as he slipped the denim and lace down her legs to her feet. When she stepped out of them, he straightened and stood back, caressing her with his heated gaze.

"You're...perfect," he said, taking her into his arms.

The feel of having all barriers between them removed, the excitement of skin against skin, caused every nerve in her body to tingle to life. Gasping from the intense desire coursing through her, Taylor wrapped her arms around Lane's waist to keep from melting into a puddle.

"Let's lie down," he said, kissing her collarbone.

When he pulled back the covers, she got into bed and marveled at how sensual the black satin sheets felt against her bare skin. It seemed to heighten the anticipation of what they were about to do. As she watched Lane remove a foil packet from the bedside table and tuck it under his pillow, she shivered from the wave of desire that swept through her.

"We're going to go slow," he said, stretching out on the bed beside her. Reaching to draw her to him, he sealed their lips in a kiss so poignant that it stole her breath. "And I'm going to try to make this as easy for you as I can, babe. But I'm afraid our lovemaking tonight won't be as pleasant for you as it will be the next time we make love."

"I know it can't be helped," she said truthfully. "But I also know you'll do everything you can to ease the discomfort."

Even though she'd had her doubts about him in the beginning, she knew it was true. The realization might have disturbed her if she'd had the time to think about it, but Lane was too busy creating a need in her like no other.

"You have no idea how much your trust means to me," he said, his eyes darkening to a deep coffee-brown.

Lowering his head, he kissed his way from the pulse at the base of her throat to the valley between her breasts and Taylor lost the ability to think. At the moment, she was too caught up in the way Lane was making her feel.

As he nipped and teased his way down her abdomen to her navel, the exquisite fluttering in the most feminine part of her transformed into the empty ache of desire and she knew for certain it was one only Lane could satisfy. But when he slid his palm over her hip, then down her thigh and back up to touch her intimately, she felt as if she would burn to a cinder.

"P-please…Lane."

"Does that feel good, Taylor?" he asked, rising up on one elbow to stare down at her.

"Y-yes…but it's making…me crazy," she said, grasping the sheet on either side of her.

"Do you want me to stop?" He kissed her and held her close as he continued his gentle stroking.

"N-no…I need…"

Her voice trailed off as she felt waves of pleasure begin to course through her. Moaning, she moved restlessly against him as the delicious sensations spread to every part of her being then slowly released her from the tension, allowing her to float back to reality.

"I've got you, Taylor," he whispered as he kissed the hollow below her ear.

"T-that was…amazing," she said, trying to catch her breath.

"I wanted to make sure you experienced some degree of pleasure this first time," he said, smiling. "That's just a glimpse of the way it will feel when we make love again."

Her chest swelled with emotion. Lane was one of the most giving men she'd ever known and she couldn't believe she hadn't seen it before now.

Placing her hands on his lean cheeks, she kissed him. "Thank you, Lane." She felt his body stir against her leg and she knew his need was as great as hers had been.

"I'm going to love you now," he said, reaching beneath his pillow for the foil packet. He quickly removed the condom, arranged their protection, then nudged her knees apart and rose over her. "I promise I'll be as gentle as I can, babe."

"I know," she said, closing her eyes and bracing herself for the unknown.

"Open your eyes, Taylor," he commanded as he positioned himself to enter her.

When she did as he directed, the look on his face caused her body to tingle and her heart to beat double time. He eased his body forward with such tenderness in his expression that she was robbed of the ability to think, much less worry about any discomfort she might feel.

As his blunt tip slowly slid into her, Lane held her gaze with his. When he breached her barrier, she barely noticed. So caught up in the moment was she that she only experienced mild discomfort when he sank into her completely and gathered her to him.

Kissing her, he asked, "Are you okay?"

She nodded. The renewed desire filling her due to the intimacy they were sharing rendered her speechless.

"I'd like to give you more time to adjust." His voice sounded strained and she could hear the toll his restraint was taking on him. "But I've wanted you since the night we met, babe."

"And I want you again, too," she admitted softly.

"I'll try to be gentle," he said as he began to rock softly against her.

She immediately responded and in no time, Taylor felt herself climbing toward the pinnacle of fulfillment. But this time the feeling was different. Having Lane deep inside of her, his body coaxing hers to join him in the wonderment of the moment, was her undoing. Clinging to him to keep from being lost, she gave in to the need he created within her. Once again, she experienced the amazement of complete release.

A moment later, she felt Lane grow still before he thrust into her one final time. As he groaned her name, his body pulsed and she knew he had found his own relief from the delicious tension.

When he collapsed on top of her, she wrapped her arms around his shoulders and held him to her. She had never met anyone as selfless as Lane or as patient. He had done everything he possibly could to make her first time a pleasurable experience. And at no small cost to himself. She'd seen the strain on his handsome face and knew he had put off his own satisfaction until she could find hers.

"Are you okay?" he asked when he finally raised his head. "I tried not to—"

"Really, I'm fine," she interrupted. "That was wonderful." She kissed his shoulder. "You were wonderful."

Levering himself to her side, he wrapped his arms around her and pulled her to him. "Thank you."

"What for?"

"For trusting me to be the first man to touch you and make love to you," he said, sounding as if he truly meant what he said.

With her head pillowed on his shoulder, she kissed his lean jaw. "I'm glad I waited," she admitted. She started to add that she was glad she had waited for him, but the thought startled her.

Why *had* she given herself to him? Why had she been willing to trust Lane with her body when she still wasn't entirely certain he hadn't somehow manipulated her grandfather?

In her heart, she knew why she had given herself to Lane after resisting temptation for years. Making love with him had felt natural and right. She didn't want to think about what that might mean. She wasn't sure she was ready for the answers.

But as she drifted off to sleep, she knew that if she was honest with herself, she would have to admit she was starting to fall for Lane and there didn't seem to be anything she could do to stop it. More importantly, she didn't really want to.

Seven

The following morning when Lane came downstairs for breakfast, he didn't hesitate to walk up behind Taylor, wrap his arms around her waist and kiss the hollow beneath her ear. "How are you feeling this morning?" he asked, loving the way her lithe body felt aligned with his.

She set down the mixing bowl she had been holding and turned to face him, her smile causing a serious hitch in his breathing. "I'm wonderful." She raised up on tiptoe to give him a quick kiss. "But I'm afraid breakfast is going to be a little late. It seems that someone kept me up last night and I ended up oversleeping this morning."

"I slept pretty well myself," he admitted, nodding. After they made love, he'd held her close and enjoyed the first good night's sleep he'd had in almost two weeks. "In fact, I slept so well, I think we should try the same arrangement tonight."

He felt a shiver course through her. "Is lovemaking always that amazing?" she asked, melting against him.

His body responded to hers so quickly that it took a moment for him to find his voice. How could he tell her that he'd never experienced anything as exciting or meaningful as what they'd shared together? Or that he had a feeling he never would experience the same with any other woman? It wasn't something he had allowed himself to think about because he wasn't sure he was ready for the answers.

"It's only going to get better, babe," he answered evasively.

Her eyes widened. "Really?"

Before he could reply, the phone rang. "This early it has to be one of my crazy-ass brothers," he said, kissing the tip of her nose. "I'll take it in the study."

As he walked down the hall, Lane decided that he wasn't all that upset by the interruption. He needed to give some serious thought to why he felt Taylor was the only woman who could excite him in ways he'd never dreamed possible.

"Talk to me, T.J.," he said, after checking the caller ID.

"You sound like you just drew an inside straight," T.J. said, laughing. "I guess you got everything settled with your new partner, huh?"

"Not exactly." Lane hesitated a moment before he

admitted, "We'll be playing a game of poker for control of the ranch in another week or so."

"Well, something has you in a good mood. You sound like you just got la—" T.J. grew quiet and Lane knew his brother had figured out why he was in such a good mood. "You do know you're playing with fire, don't you, bro?"

"Don't worry about me," Lane said, irritated by his brother's perceptiveness. "What did you need?"

"Uh-oh."

"What?" Lane demanded.

"You're pissed off. That tells me there's more going on than just a little friendly fun with your business partner," T.J. said knowingly. "So when do we get to meet the future Mrs. Donaldson?"

"Shut up and tell me why you called or I'm going to hang up," Lane snapped. He loved his brother, but he suspected that T.J.'s observations were hitting too close to home.

"All right, all right. Simmer down, Freud. I've got a heap of trouble brewing with that woman next door. Her stallion keeps jumping the fence to romance my mares and I need you guys to help me out," T.J. said, his voice tight with anger.

"How many more of your brood mares has he bred this time?" Lane asked, understanding his brother's frustration. T.J. raised championship reining horses and having a rogue stallion impregnate his brood stock would cost him hundreds of thousands of dollars and set his breeding program back several years.

"He covered four more of my mares yesterday before

I discovered him in the pasture," T.J. said disgustedly. "That makes ten in the past four months."

"What can the guys and I do to help?" Lane asked, knowing he and his brothers would all drop whatever they were doing to help out T.J.

Over the past year or so, T.J. had tried talking to the woman about checking and mending her fences more often. When that failed, he had requested that she keep the stud on another part of her ranch. Since that hadn't netted the desired result, it appeared that he'd come up with another plan.

"I figure with the six of us and my two hired hands, we can get a six-foot-tall woven-wire fence put up between my place and hers by nightfall," T.J. said determinedly.

"That should take care of your problem," Lane agreed. "I'll be there right after breakfast."

"Thanks, Lane," T.J. said sincerely. "I owe you one."

"See you in about two hours," Lane added, ending the call.

As he walked back into the kitchen, Taylor had just set two plates of eggs Benedict with smoked salmon, hash browns and fresh mixed fruit at their places at the table. "It looks delicious," he said, holding her chair for her. "I haven't eaten this well in years."

"Just wait until you see what I plan for dinner," she said, smiling.

"I'm afraid I'll probably be late for dinner tonight," he said, taking a drink of the freshly squeezed orange juice by his plate. "My brothers and I are going to help

T.J. put up a boundary fence between his place and another ranch today."

"Is he having problems with his neighbor?" she asked, sounding genuinely interested.

Telling her about the woman's stallion and the cost to T.J.'s breeding program, he gave her an apologetic smile. "I'm sorry, but I won't be able to help you practice playing poker today, either."

"Don't worry about that," she said, placing her soft hand on his forearm. "I realize how important it is to stop the neighbor's horse from visiting your brother's mares. I'll just plan to have dinner ready a couple of hours later than usual."

Lane took hold of her hand and scooted his chair back so he could pull her over to sit on his lap. "I promise I'll be back as soon as I can."

She kissed him and he thought he might go up in a puff of smoke at the need the simple caress created within him. "While you're helping your brother, I'm going to call the shipping company and find out where my things are. They should have been here at the end of last week. If I can run them down, I'm going to spend the day putting everything away."

"So you're that sure you're going to win the big game?" he teased.

Grinning, she nodded. "I'm going to knock your socks off."

"You accomplished that last night, babe." He kissed her, then set her on her feet and rose from his chair. "I think I'd better get going."

"But you haven't finished breakfast," she said, looking at the uneaten food on his plate.

"As delicious as I know those eggs would be, what I'd really like to have isn't on the menu," he said, going over to the cabinet to get a travel mug to fill with coffee.

"I could make you something different," she said, looking a bit uncertain.

Walking back over to her, he set the mug on the table and took her in his arms. "What I want for breakfast involves you and me, upstairs with our clothes off," he said, kissing her soundly. When he raised his head, he gazed down into her passion-glazed emerald eyes. "But I have work to do, and I can't afford to get distracted. I'll see you this evening, Taylor."

Forcing himself to put one boot in front of the other, he grabbed his hat from the peg beside the door and walked out of the house without looking back. He had to. Otherwise, he would have carried her upstairs and spent the entire day making love to the woman who was quickly becoming as important to him as his next breath.

His heart hammered hard against his rib cage as he climbed into his truck and started the engine. Now he definitely knew he needed some time away from Taylor in order to do a little self-analysis and figure out what the hell he was going to do about the feelings he'd discovered.

Taylor alternated between outright fury and fear as she waited for Lane to return home. By the time she saw his headlights cut through the darkness as his truck came down the road leading to the house, she was surprised she hadn't worn a trench in the hardwood floor from her pacing. Deciding not to wait until he came into the house, she unlocked the back door, marched out onto the porch and down the steps.

"We have a problem," she said when he opened the driver's door. As angry as she was, relief flowed through her at the sight of him. Now that Lane was home, she felt safer and more secure than she had the entire day.

"What's wrong?" he asked, getting out of the truck.

"It's Roy Lee," she said, unable to keep from shuddering. Just saying the man's name gave her a case of the creeps.

"Are you all right?" Lane demanded, placing his hands on her shoulders.

His concern was touching, but at the moment she needed to tell him what had happened. "We have to fire Roy Lee Wilks," she stated flatly.

"Why?" Lane's eyes narrowed, making him look dangerous. "What's he done this time?"

"He stole all of the things I shipped from California." Every time she thought of what the cowboy had done, a fresh wave of anger burned through her. "When I called the shipping company, I was told that they had delivered the containers last week and Roy Lee was the one who signed for them."

"What did he do with them?" Lane asked, propping his fists on his hips and turning to stare hard at the bunkhouse.

"I don't know." She shook her head. "I haven't talked to him about it."

"I'm glad you didn't confront him," Lane said, putting his arms around her and pulling her to his chest.

"I wanted to talk to you first and see how you thought I should handle it," she admitted.

"You're not going to take care of this," he said firmly. "I am."

She frowned. "But it was my things he took. I should be the one to talk to him about it."

"I understand that you want to have your say and I respect that," he said, as if choosing his words carefully. "But in this case, I wouldn't advise it." When she started to protest, he held up one hand to stop her. "Consider this. Roy Lee's behavior wouldn't, by any stretch of the imagination, be considered stable. I'm not saying he's dangerous, but that's one chance I'm not willing to take."

"What are you going to do?" she asked, suddenly concerned that they might be dealing with more than she'd realized.

"I'm going over to the bunkhouse to find out where Roy Lee put your things, then I'm going to tell him to pack his gear and get off the property," Lane answered. He pointed toward the house. "I want you to go inside and lock the door."

"I've had them locked all day, even though I knew he was working away from the house with the other men," she admitted.

He nodded. "Go on inside while I take care of getting rid of Roy Lee."

"Be careful," she said as a shudder ran through her.

"Don't worry about me, babe. I'll be fine." He gave her a quick kiss. "I may not be in for a while. I'm going to make sure Roy Lee gets everything packed and loaded into his truck. Then I'm going to see that he drives away."

An hour later, Taylor breathed a sigh of relief when Lane used his keys to let himself into the house. "Did you have any trouble getting Roy Lee to leave?" she asked, walking over to wrap her arms around Lane's waist. His arms immediately closed around her and pulled her close.

"No. At first, he tried to talk his way out of it, but when I told him we knew that he had signed for the boxes, he explained that he stored them in the hayloft in the barn." Lane shook his head. "He was waiting for a chance to bring them to you when I wasn't around."

"I don't like the sound of that," she said, snuggling against his solid chest.

"He wanted to ask you to go dancing with him and decided that he'd have a better chance of you agreeing if you thought he'd found your missing things." Sounding tired, Lane finished, "Roy Lee is socially awkward and clearly has a few issues with reasoning, but I still don't think he meant any harm. He was just trying to impress you because of a deep infatuation."

"Is that your professional opinion?" she asked, leaning back to look up at him.

He grinned. "Sure, if you want to call it that."

For the first time since he had returned from helping his brother, she noticed how exhausted he looked. "I'm so sorry you had to deal with this, Lane, especially after such a long day. You look like you're ready to drop in your tracks. I'm afraid I was too upset to make the dinner I had planned, but while you take a shower, I could make some sandwiches for us."

"That sounds good," he said, yawning. He kissed her forehead, then stepped back to unsnap his sleeves and the front of his shirt. "I won't be long."

While Lane went upstairs, Taylor set to work and in no time had several sandwiches prepared for them. When she looked at the clock on the stove, she frowned. Lane should have finished with his shower and been back downstairs by now.

Deciding to check on him and find out what was keeping him, she headed to his bedroom. She started to knock on his door and discovered it was partially open. "Lane?"

Her heart skipped several beats when she found him lying on the bed sound asleep beside his clean clothes. His nude body was every bit as magnificent as she remembered from the night before and even completely relaxed, his physique was impressive.

Taylor's chest filled with an emotion she was determined to ignore as she moved his clothes, then reached to pull the comforter over him. He had been thoroughly exhausted from working on his brother's fence all day, yet when he returned home he had insisted on coming to her rescue and dealing with Roy Lee.

Quietly leaving the room, she went back downstairs to the kitchen. She wrapped and put away the sandwiches she'd made in the refrigerator, then she cleaned the kitchen. After checking the door to make sure it was locked, she turned out the light and headed back upstairs. When she reached the doors to their bedrooms, she looked from one to the other. She knew where she should sleep. But that wasn't where she wanted to be.

Entering her bedroom, she changed into a nightshirt, then walked across the hall, entered Lane's room and climbed into bed beside him. Even in sleep, he turned toward her to put his arm over her.

She refused to dwell on why it seemed so right to be sleeping in his arms. It was where she wanted to be and felt as natural as taking her next breath. Besides, she was tired of fighting what she had suspected for the past couple of days. Whether she wanted it to be true or not, she was falling head over heels for Lane Donaldson.

Three days after the incident with Roy Lee, Lane found himself taking a deep fortifying breath as he parked his truck beside his brothers' and got out to walk around and open the passenger door for Taylor. Facing an entire day of listening to his brothers rib him about his relationship with his new business partner was about as appealing as trying to climb a barbed-wire fence buck naked. But there hadn't been any question about him attending the family dinner to welcome his new niece, nor had he considered—not even for a second— not bringing Taylor with him to the gathering.

"I hope the gift I got for the baby is something they need," she said when he helped her down from the truck.

"They'll love it," he said, knowing Ryder and Summer would be extremely appreciative of Taylor's thoughtfulness. He and his brothers had all done well after college and had become extremely wealthy, but thanks to their foster father, they had their priorities straight. They remembered what was important in life.

As they walked across the yard, he could tell that Taylor was apprehensive about meeting his family. He could understand her insecurities. But she had nothing to fear. They were going to love her just as much as...he did?

His heart stalled and he wasn't sure he'd ever breathe again.

Where the hell had that come from? And why of all times did it have to occur to him right now?

"Lane, are you all right?" Taylor asked, her concern evident.

"Uh, yeah, I'm fine," he finally managed, even though he was struggling to assimilate his new self-awareness.

"Hey there, bro!" Nate called from the gathering of men on the covered patio. "We've got a beer over here with your name on it."

"Glad you could make it, Lane," Ryder said, walking over to them.

"You know I wouldn't miss it," Lane answered.

Completely ignoring Lane, his brother turned toward Taylor. "We talked on the phone the morning my little Katie was born and I'm happy to finally meet you. I'm Ryder McClain, this big lug's better-looking brother."

"You wish," Lane shot back, forcing a grin.

He would just have to deal with the discovery about his newfound feelings later. Right now, he needed to concentrate on hiding them before one of the other men figured out what was going on with him. And there wasn't a doubt in his mind that if he wasn't careful, one of them would. That was one of the hazards of knowing each other so well.

"Nice to see you again, Taylor." Nate laughed as he handed Lane a bottle of beer. "And don't listen to these two sidewinders. They both know I'm better-looking than the two of them combined."

"That's just what we let you think, Nate," T.J. said, stepping forward. "Hi, Taylor. I'm T.J."

When he shifted the baby in his arms to his shoulder, Sam smiled and nodded. "I'm Sam and this is my son, little Hank. We're all happy you decided to join our celebration."

"Thank you for inviting me," Taylor said, smiling. "It's nice getting to know all of you."

"Sam, do you want me to take little Hank and get him down for a nap? Dinner will be ready in about ten minutes," Bria said from the back door. When she noticed Taylor standing beside him, she smiled. "Lane, why didn't you show Taylor inside? I'm sure she'd rather talk to me, Summer and Mariah than listen to you men discuss your cattle or argue about which bucking bull you think will be champion this year."

Placing his hand on her back, Lane walked Taylor over to the door. "Taylor this is Sam's wife, Bria. She's the glue that holds us all together." He kissed Bria's cheek. "We all love her for it, too."

"Come on inside," Bria said, hugging Taylor. She took the baby from her husband and motioned for Taylor to follow her. "I'll introduce you to my sister, Mariah, and Ryder's wife, Summer."

As Bria took Taylor inside to get acquainted with the other two women, Lane rejoined his brothers. Looking around, he asked, "Where's Jaron?"

Ryder nodded toward the road. "Here he comes now."

When Jaron parked and got out of his truck, they all greeted him much like they'd greeted Lane.

"Mariah is in the house with the other women if you want to go in and tell her you're here, Jaron," Sam said, grinning from ear to ear.

"Stuff it, Rafferty," Jaron shot back as he accepted the beer T.J. handed him. "She's probably still pissed off at me anyway."

"If you don't stop dragging your ass and ask that girl out, you're going to miss your chance," Nate advised.

"Is that what happened when you stopped seeing that little blonde down in Waco?" Jaron asked, giving Nate a knowing look.

"That's different and you know it," Nate said, his expression turning serious. Glaring at Jaron, he shook his head. "That was a low blow and not something I expected from my best friend."

Lane and the other four men looked from one brother to the other. Jaron and Nate had been best friends since meeting at the Last Chance Ranch and they still traveled the rodeo circuit together. Their personalities were completely different, but they had always seemed to balance each other out. While Jaron was quiet and brooding, Nate was outgoing and rarely encountered a situation he couldn't joke his way out of. Nate could always bring Jaron out of his shell and Jaron helped keep Nate grounded. But this was the first time any of them had seen tension between the two men.

"Look, I'm sorry, Nate," Jaron apologized, looking contrite. "It's just that I don't want to talk about Mariah. I'm too old for her and that's that."

Nate nodded. "Apology accepted, bro."

"Here we go again," T.J. said, shaking his head. "Methuselah is back to his old self."

Just when Lane thought he was in the clear and wouldn't have to dodge his brothers' questions or listen to their good-natured speculation about his relationship with Taylor, Ryder asked, "So what's the story with you and Taylor?"

"Yeah, when are you supposed to play the poker game that will decide which one of you gets control of the Lucky Ace?" Sam asked.

"I'll be setting that up for next week," Lane answered, glancing toward the house. What was taking so long for the women to call them in for dinner?

"You know there is a way for both of you to keep the ranch," T.J. said, rocking back on his heels.

Lane knew where his brother was going with that train of thought and he didn't care for it one damned bit. "I'm not going to marry the woman just to keep the ranch."

"So you'll marry her for other reasons?" Ryder asked, laughing.

Taking a swig of his beer, Lane almost choked. "I don't ever expect to get married."

"Never say never, bro," Ryder said, tempting Lane

to wipe away his brother's ear-to-ear grin with a good right hook. "If you'll remember, I said that just before I woke up and figured out that Summer was the best thing that ever happened to me." He laughed. "After that, I couldn't put my ring on her finger fast enough."

"That was different," Lane said stubbornly, shaking his head.

"I've got a hundred bucks that says Lane and Taylor are married by the Fourth of July," T.J. said, laughing like a damned hyena.

"I say it'll be next month," Nate said, digging in his pocket for the money to place his bet.

"I'll take Labor Day," Jaron stated.

"Who's going to take care of the prize pool?" Sam asked.

"I'll hold onto it," Ryder volunteered.

While his brothers placed their bets on when they thought he and Taylor would be tying the knot, Lane checked his watch. Groaning, he shook his head. He and Taylor hadn't been there more than thirty minutes and his brothers already had them walking down the aisle. No doubt about it. It was going to be one of the longest evenings of his life.

After dinner, Taylor laughed as she watched the five proud uncles argue over who would be the first to hold their new niece.

"I'm the most experienced at holding a baby," Sam said, his tone practical. "I think that makes me the obvious choice."

"Yeah, but I have a way with females," Nate argued. "If she starts to cry, I can charm her into a good mood."

T.J. rolled his eyes as he shook his head. "That goofy grin of yours would scare the bejesus out of her. I should be the one to hold little Katie first."

"What makes you say that, T.J.?" Jaron asked, frowning. "You can't even get along with that neighbor lady of yours. What makes you think you can do any better with a baby girl?"

As she watched the men argue their cases, Taylor noticed Lane quietly scoot his chair back, rise to his feet and walk to the head of the table to take the baby from Ryder. "You all just keep on arguing," Lane said, sounding smug as he cradled the infant to his broad chest. "In the meantime, I'm going to get acquainted with our new niece."

"Now see what you did?" Nate complained to T.J. "Lane's getting to hold Katie first."

"Me?" T.J. shook his head. "I didn't do anything. You were the one…"

While the two brothers bickered good-naturedly, Taylor's pulse skipped a beat as she watched Lane with the tiny pink bundle in his arms. Unlike a lot of men, he looked completely natural and at ease holding the baby. What was there about a big, strong man gently holding an infant that melted a woman's heart? More importantly, why was her chest tightening with emotion?

She had never given having children a second thought, nor had she ever thought a baby would be in her future. But something about watching Lane with the little girl had her wondering what it would be like to see him holding their baby.

Her heart stalled and she had to set her iced tea glass back on the table to keep from dropping it. What in the world had brought that thought to mind? She wasn't actually daydreaming of becoming *that* involved with Lane, was she?

When he looked up to see her watching him, his smile made her catch her breath. "Taylor, have you had the chance to hold little Katie yet?"

"N-no," she said, shaking her head. "Your brothers should have their turn first."

"We don't mind." Nate spoke up, smiling. "Ladies first."

"That's right," T.J. agreed. "We'll all have our chance and before you know it, she'll have us wrapped around her little finger just like little Hank does."

To Taylor's utter disbelief, Lane walked over and placed the infant in her arms, then sat down in the chair at the dining room table beside her. "I'm going to be her favorite uncle," he stated, resting his arm along the back of her chair.

"I've never held a baby before," she said, marveling at how tiny and sweet the child was.

"Never?" Bria asked, her tone filled with disbelief.

"I don't have siblings and none of my friends have children," Taylor answered as she gazed down at the sleeping little girl. "This is nice."

When she looked up to see the smile on Lane's face, a warm feeling spread throughout her body. "You're a natural," he whispered, tenderly touching the baby's tiny hand.

"Now we know who to call when little Hank is fussy and I'm busy with the livestock and you're trying to fix supper, Bria," Sam said, laughing.

"I'll put the Lucky Ace's number on speed dial with Mariah's." Bria laughed as she rose to take her and her husband's plates into the kitchen.

"Taylor, it looks like you and I have found ourselves a couple of babysitting jobs," Mariah said with a laugh.

"There's only one problem," Taylor said, nodding. "Beyond holding a baby, I don't know the first thing about taking care of one."

Summer smiled as she confided, "I didn't either until Katie was born. Thank goodness for motherly instincts. Not to mention all the parenting sites on the internet."

When little Hank started making discontented noises from his baby carrier, Bria handed Sam a baby bottle. "Why don't you men take the babies into the family room? After you feed little Hank you can all argue over who gets to hold the munchkins while we clean up the kitchen."

Taylor handed the newborn back to Lane as she rose from her chair to help the women clear the table. As she watched them file out of the dining room, she couldn't help but feel envious of the closeness they all shared. They might have started out on a rocky path in life, but the men had bonded into a family that was as strong and loving as any she had ever seen.

"I noticed that you and Jaron still aren't speaking,"

Summer said to Mariah as Taylor entered the kitchen. "You still haven't forgiven him?"

"Nope." Mariah shook her head. "He shouldn't have gloated over being right about little Hank's gender."

"Don't you think you've punished him enough?" Bria asked.

"I want a formal apology," Mariah insisted. "Until I get that, I have nothing to say to Jaron."

"She's been in love with Jaron since she was a teenager and I suspect he's in love with her," Summer whispered to Taylor. "But he has some crazy idea that he's too old for her."

"I noticed that he couldn't take his eyes off of her during dinner," Taylor admitted.

Summer nodded. "It's that way every time we get together."

"Maybe one day they'll work it out," Taylor offered.

"Maybe," Summer said, smiling.

As talk turned to babies, breast-feeding schedules and the lack of sleep both new mothers were experiencing, Taylor smiled. Even the wives of the men were close, making the blended family all the more special.

Several hours later as they drove away from Ryder and Summer's ranch, Taylor glanced over at Lane. "I love your family," she said, sincerely. "Everyone is so friendly and nice. I really enjoyed getting to know them."

"I'm lucky to have them." Lane shrugged. "Even though there are times I'd like to muzzle them to shut them up, there isn't one of them that wouldn't be there for me in a heartbeat if I needed them, the same as I will always be there for them."

"I think it's wonderful that you all have stayed so close over the years." She had friends, but the bond between the men she'd met tonight went beyond friendship. They had chosen to become a family and were closer than some people she knew who were related by blood. "I would have loved to have a family that got along that well."

Reaching across the truck's console, he covered her hand with his. "We're just like any other family. Most of the time we get along. But other times it can be a zoo," he said, smiling. "Just because you see us getting along, don't think that we don't have our arguments sometimes."

"But you always get over it and you're right back to getting along?" she guessed.

"Always," he admitted.

"That's something my parents never do," she said, sighing. "They just continue to shout at each other."

"But they love you," Lane said gently.

She nodded. "I guess everyone has a different family dynamic," she admitted. "Some are just more harmonious than others."

Staring out the windshield at the star-studded night sky, Taylor still couldn't help but be envious of Lane's family. Besides the fact that they all got along so well, listening to Bria and Summer talk about their husbands almost made Taylor wish she could have a relationship like that.

She had never entertained the idea of getting married and starting a family because of her parents and their hostilities toward each other. But seeing Lane's brothers and their wives and the loving way they treated each other was eye-opening for her. It had shown her what a relationship based on love and respect could be like.

"I'll be setting up the poker game over in Shreveport for the end of this coming week," Lane said, breaking into her musings.

"Do you think I'm ready to match my skills against yours?" She wasn't overly thrilled by the news. For one thing, she wasn't entirely certain she would be a worthy opponent. And for another, no matter who won, the other would be leaving the ranch. So why did that make her sad?

Over two weeks ago, all she'd wanted—all she could think about—was winning back his half of the ranch and ordering Lane off the property. But now?

"You still have to watch your tells," he answered. "But yes, you're ready to play me for the ranch."

They were both quiet for the rest of the drive and by the time Lane parked his truck next to the Lucky Ace ranch house, Taylor decided not to think about what would happen when they played poker for the ranch. She was determined to enjoy whatever time they had left together.

"I don't know about you, but I'm damned glad to be home," he said, giving her a look that caused her insides to feel as if they had turned to warm pudding. "I think turning in early would be a good idea."

"Really? I thought you told your brothers you were going to come home and watch the baseball game," she said, feigning innocence. She knew exactly what he meant and her heart sped up at the thought of once again being loved by him.

"What I tell my brothers and what I do are sometimes two different things," he said, getting out of the truck to come around and help her from the passenger side. Putting his arm around her shoulders, he leaned down to whisper close to her ear as they walked to the porch. "I would much rather take you upstairs and hit a home run than watch some overpaid athlete only make it to second or third base."

"Don't you think the Rangers will score at least once or twice tonight?" she teased.

Laughing, he shook his head. "Not the kind of scoring I intend to do when we go upstairs, babe."

"Oh, so you intend to race around the bases?" she asked as they entered the house.

He locked the door behind them and immediately took her into his arms. "Not a chance. I have every intention of taking things slow and enjoying every base I touch." He kissed her until she felt as if her limbs had been replaced by limp spaghetti. "And I'm going to make sure you enjoy every one of them, too."

Eight

Taking Taylor by the hand, Lane led her across the foyer and up the stairs. He had spent a miserable afternoon and evening checking his watch to see how much longer it would be before he could whisk her away from his family and bring her home to make love to her.

When they reached his room, he walked over and lit a group of candles he had placed on the nightstand before they left to go to Ryder's. "I'm going to make this a night you'll never forget," he said, turning to put his arms around her.

"You've got my attention," she said, rising up on her tiptoes to kiss him. "What do you have in mind?"

"You'll see," he answered as he pulled off his boots and unbuttoned his white oxford-cloth shirt. When she started to take off her blue silk blouse, he shook his head. "I want the pleasure of doing that for you."

After quickly stripping off the rest of his clothes, he knelt to remove her shoes. He caressed her slender ankles and massaged the arches of her bare feet. He had every intention of taking his time to touch every part of her delightful body and build the energy within her.

As he reached for the buttons on her shirt, he smiled. "I want you to close your eyes and concentrate on how I'm making you feel while I take off your clothes."

"All right," she murmured as she did as he commanded.

Releasing the top button, he kissed her satiny skin down to the next button and then the next. By the time he reached the waistband of her navy linen slacks, she had goose bumps and he was certain they weren't from cold.

"You're…driving me…crazy," she said, sounding delightfully breathless.

He put his index finger to her lips as he whispered close to her ear. "Shh. I want you to promise you'll keep your eyes closed and won't talk. I want you to get lost in the way I make you feel. Okay?"

When she nodded, he slipped the garment from her shoulders, then took his time kissing her arms—from her shoulders to the tips of her fingers—before he reached for the clasp of her bra. Unfastening the satin and lace, then tossing it aside, he used his palms to support her full breasts as he kissed one hardened nipple while he chafed the other with the pad of his thumb. By the time he finished giving his full attention to both tight tips, a tiny moan escaped her perfect lips.

"Let me hear you, Taylor," he whispered, skimming her satiny skin with his lips.

Without saying another word, he unbuttoned her slacks and slowly slid the zipper down, kissing his way along her lower belly much the way he'd done when he removed her shirt. When he reached the waistband of her bikini panties he stopped to slide her slacks down, then kissed her from her thighs all the way to her ankles. Kissing his way back up along the inside of her legs, he paused to remove the scrape of lace between him and his goal.

"Lane?"

"You promised," he said, kissing her intimately.

When she moaned and began to sway, he caught her hands in his to place them on his shoulders. As he continued his sensual assault, her nails scored his skin and he knew she had almost reached her limit.

Rising to his feet, Lane swung her up in his arms and carried her over to the bed. His body burned to make her his once more, but this night wasn't about him. It was all about Taylor and bringing her the most pleasure a man could give to the woman who owned his heart.

If he had given himself enough time to think about that and what it meant, he might have run like hell. But he concentrated on the woman in his arms as he placed her on the bed, then he reached for a foil packet from the drawer in the nightstand.

When he had their protection in place, he sat on the bed beside her and lifted her to straddle him. He gritted his teeth as he eased her down onto him and she slowly took him in.

"Open your eyes, Taylor," he commanded. When she did, the passion in the emerald depths robbed him of breath.

Taking her hand in his, he placed it over his heart while at the same time he covered her heart with his palm. "I want you to feel our hearts beat while I make love to you."

As they stared into each other's eyes, he urged her to wrap her legs around him and begin a slow rocking motion against him. Without hesitation she moved her body with his and in no time their hearts united to beat as one. In time with the rhythm of their lovemaking, the beat increased along with their movements. As the tension built, Lane knew that they were both reaching the summit they both sought.

With hearts pounding to the same cadence, her body clenched him tightly and he felt them both let go and give in to the release of complete fulfillment. Feeling as if he might pass out, Lane held her to him as they rode out the storm of pleasure engulfing them.

As the last waves of passion coursed through them, he knew beyond a shadow of doubt that the woman in his arms had changed his life forever. She had not only drained him of every ounce of energy he possessed, she had just taken away his will to fight his feelings any longer. He was in love with her and as soon as they settled ownership of the ranch, he fully intended to tell her.

The following morning at breakfast, Taylor smiled when Lane twined their fingers on top of the table. He seemed to take every opportunity to touch and kiss her. And she loved every single minute of it.

"What do you have planned for today?" she asked as she took a sip of her coffee.

"Right after I set up the poker game, I'll be helping Judd in the north pasture," he answered, giving her a smile that caused her pulse to take off at a full gallop. "He needs somebody to help him cut several cows from one of the herds and bring them up to the holding pen."

"Why? Is something wrong with them?" she asked, knowing they sometimes separated cattle from the herds because of a health issue.

Lane nodded. "He noticed some cattle yesterday that looked like they might be coming down with pinkeye."

"That's highly contagious," she said, remembering hearing her grandfather talk about how the disease could be passed on to the entire herd if the infected cows weren't separated and treated immediately.

"We'll get it taken care of," he assured her.

"Why isn't one of the other men helping him?" she asked, knowing they had several cowboys working for them.

"After we fired Roy Lee, we're a man short," he explained. He rose from the table to take his breakfast plate to the sink for rinsing, then put it into the dishwasher. "Besides, Judd knows I'm pretty good at roping and thought I might come in handy if one of the cows is reluctant to go into the chute on her own."

Joining him at the sink, she wrapped her arms around his waist to give him a hug. "Should I plan on you being back for lunch?"

"I wouldn't count on it," he said, kissing her until

she felt completely breathless. "But I'll definitely be here for dinner."

He kissed her again, then grabbed his hat and walked out of the house. Standing there watching him leave, she couldn't help but wonder what would happen when they played the poker game to decide who would control the ranch.

If he won would he be opposed to the idea of her staying longer than they had agreed on? Or in the event that she won, would his pride allow him to accept her invitation to remain on the ranch until the attraction between them ran its course?

Starting the dishwasher, she finished cleaning up the kitchen and started upstairs to unpack some of the cartons Lane had rescued from the hayloft in the barn. She was optimistically going to unpack her clothes and the few personal items she had shipped to herself with the hope that things would work out no matter who won the game.

Three hours later, Taylor came back downstairs to take a break and had just made herself a mocha latte when someone knocked on the front door. She had no idea who the visitor could be, unless it was one of Lane's brothers or their wives. Either way, she'd enjoyed talking to them the night before and a visit from any of them would be more than welcome.

But when she opened the door, Roy Lee Wilks stood on the other side. "Good morning, Ms. Scott," he said, taking his sweat-stained hat off in a gentlemanly manner.

"What are you doing here, Roy Lee?" she demanded.

"I thought Lane told you to clear off the property and not come back."

He nodded. "I'm real sorry about taking your stuff like I did, but I wanted to bring it to you myself." A dark scowl replaced his friendly expression. "He ruined that idea."

"Okay, fine. Apology accepted." Deciding not to tell the man that she had been the one who'd discovered what he had done, she pointed to Roy Lee's truck. "Now please leave and don't come back."

She started to close the door, but he wedged his boot against it. "Telling you I'm sorry is only part of the reason I'm here," he said, removing some papers from the hip pocket of his jeans. His expression turned outright nasty. "I just thought you'd like to know a few things about the son of a bitch you're playing house with. I've seen the two of you cozied up together here on the porch and you don't have any idea what kind of man he is."

"You were watching us?" Outraged, she shook her head. "Get off this property right now and don't you ever step another foot on the Lucky Ace again. If you do, I'll have you arrested for trespassing, harassment and anything else I can think of."

"Not before I give you these," he said, shoving the papers he held into her hand. "If you're smart, you'll read up on Donaldson. He's not the man you think he is. You're sure that I'm the bad guy here, but some of the things he's done makes me look like a saint."

Before she could throw the papers back at him, he moved his foot and turned to jog down the steps. He got into his truck and drove away, the tires squealing.

Her hands shook as she closed and bolted the door. Her instincts had been correct about Roy Lee. He was without a doubt one of the creepiest men she'd ever had the misfortune to meet.

Walking straight into the kitchen, she started to throw the papers he'd given her into the trash can under the sink. But something caught her eye and she closed the cabinet door instead.

The papers were copies of news articles from several of the Houston newspapers. There was one article detailing the suicide of Lane's father and his embezzlement at the financial institution where he had been employed. He had been facing years in prison for stealing his clients' money and chose to end his life rather than spend the majority of the rest of it behind bars.

Sitting down at the table, she read on and learned that Ken Donaldson's only son, thirteen-year-old Lane Donaldson, had found the man hanging from the rafters of their garage, just as Lane had told her. But the information in the next article was what caused her heart to stall and her stomach to feel as if she would become physically sick. The son of a disgraced financial advisor who had committed suicide had been arrested two years later for running confidence schemes and selling stolen goods to several pawn shops in the Houston area. Because he was a juvenile at the time, the newspaper was prohibited from releasing his name, but there was no doubt they were reporting on Lane. The article went on to say that the boy had pled guilty to the charges and because of extenuating circumstances had been placed into the custody of the foster care system instead of being detained in a juvenile detention facility. There wasn't a doubt in her mind the newspaper referred to Lane.

He had mentioned being sent to a foster care home called the Last Chance Ranch, but she had assumed the ranch name was just something someone had come up with. She hadn't believed it had a literal meaning. Apparently, she'd been wrong.

Her first instincts had been right about Lane. He must have manipulated her grandfather into wagering half of the ranch and then cheated to win the game.

Why had she let down her guard? How could she have been so gullible?

Normally, she wasn't nearly as trusting as she had been with Lane. Nor did she take everything someone said at face value. But Lane had been so convincing when he swore he wasn't guilty of the things she had accused him of doing. She knew now that he wasn't just a swindler; he was a consummate liar as well.

With her heart feeling as if it had shattered into a million pieces, she went upstairs to get her laptop and spent the rest of the day searching every newspaper archive she could find that might give her additional details about Lane and his past. There wasn't much more, other than his mother's brief obituary and the details of the real estate and personal possessions auction that was held to recover some of the money Lane's father had stolen from his clients.

But by the time Lane returned to the house after helping the ranch foreman with the sick cattle, Taylor was waiting for him, armed with all the information she needed. She felt like a fool. Over these last few weeks, she had convinced herself that she'd been wrong about him and that he was trustworthy after all. She'd even given herself to him and all the while, he was probably laughing himself silly at what an easy mark she had been.

"Did you set up the poker game?" she asked when he opened the back door and hung his hat on the peg beside it.

Opening the refrigerator to get a beer, he nodded. "I called Cole Sullivan and he's agreed to let us use the VIP poker room at the End of the Rainbow Casino on Friday." He walked over to sit at the table with her. "He said that he just heard about your grandfather and that he has something Ben left for him to give to both of us when he passed." Lane frowned. "Do you have any idea what that could be?"

"Why would I have the slightest clue what my grandfather gave to a man I've never met?" she asked, unable to keep an edge from her voice.

He reached across the table to cover her hand with his. "Is something wrong?"

"You could say that," she said, removing her hand from beneath his.

"Tell me what's bothering you, babe." He looked sincere, but she knew better than to trust him.

"First of all, I don't want you calling me 'babe' anymore," she said, folding her arms beneath her breasts. "I'm not your babe, your honey, your sweetheart or anything else."

He had his beer bottle halfway to his mouth, but he

slowly set it back on the table. "Okay. Would you like to tell me what's going on and why you suddenly take exception to my calling you that when it didn't seem to bother you before?"

"I learned something about you today that I find very disturbing," she said, forcing herself to stay calm. If she didn't keep her emotions under tight control, she knew for certain they were going to betray her. And she'd rather die than allow Lane to see how badly he had hurt her.

His eyes narrowed slightly. "What did you learn?"

She could tell he anticipated what she was about to say. He had probably already formed a plan for damage control on the outside chance that she did figure things out. But as far as she was concerned, there was nothing he could say that she would find redeeming.

"You failed to tell me that you were put into the foster care system because you were a thief and a grifter." She shook her head at her own foolishness. "I should have trusted my instincts. You did swindle my grandfather out of half of this ranch, didn't you?"

"No." He rose from his chair to walk over and pour his beer down the sink. When he turned to face her, his expression gave nothing away. "I told you before, I've never cheated at cards."

"Sure. Whatever you say. You were good enough at swindling and stealing from people that it took a year for the authorities to catch you," she said, getting up from the table to face him. "You had to have been a very convincing liar to get all those people to believe your schemes. I know you had me fooled."

"I've never lied to you," he said, taking a step toward her.

Refusing to let him intimidate her, she stood her ground. "You must think I'm horribly gullible or more likely, you think I'm a complete fool. Did you have yourself a good laugh when I made it so easy for you to seduce me?"

"It wasn't like that, Taylor," he insisted. "Deep down you have to know that."

"To tell you the truth, at the moment I don't trust myself to know anything," she admitted. "I suppose I have you to thank for teaching me that my judgment is completely unreliable and more than a little flawed."

"Listen up, Taylor. You have a flaw, all right. It's jumping to conclusions before you have all of the facts." His voice held a steely edge and there was no doubt he was furious, but he didn't shout as she'd expected him to do. He didn't have to. His deadly calm tone was far more effective. "Yes, I withheld the information about my past for two very good reasons. Number one, I'm not at all proud of it. And number two, I knew how you would react."

"Were you ever going to tell me?" she asked.

"Yes." He took a deep breath. "I intended to tell you about the trouble I got into when I was a kid, as well as my reasons for doing what I did. But I was waiting for the right time."

"Are you going to tell me now?" she asked, wondering why she bothered to ask. He probably thought she was so gullible that he could tell her anything and she would believe him.

"No, I'm not," he stated, surprising her. "You have your mind made up about me and, at the moment, there's nothing I can say that will change it. I'll tell you everything tomorrow after you've calmed down."

"There won't be an opportunity tomorrow," she said determinedly. "I want you out of my house and off my property until after we play for the ranch."

"This place is just as much mine as it is yours," he pointed out, his voice still deadly quiet.

"This is an intolerable situation and one of us has to leave," she said, hoping he wouldn't call her bluff. Legally he had every right to stay and they both knew it. "You're the obvious choice because you can go stay with one of your brothers. I don't have anyone I can turn to."

He stared at her for what seemed an eternity before he finally nodded and started toward the hallway. "I'll go pack a bag and be out of here in fifteen minutes." Turning back, he added, "But don't think I'm giving up. This is my home now and I have every intention of living here for a *very* long time."

Taylor waited until he went upstairs to gather his clothes before she walked out onto the front porch and sat down in the swing. She didn't want to watch him walk out the door and run the risk of abandoning her resolve. It would be too tempting to tell him to stay and to ask him to give her a reasonable explanation for why he had turned to a life of crime after his father died, as well as why he'd lied to her—even if it was by omission.

Nothing would make her happier than for Lane to tell her that he had only been acting out as a normal teen would do after becoming the victim of a life-altering tragedy. He had lost so much in such a short time; she couldn't imagine how traumatizing it had to have been for him to find his father's dead body. He had only been thirteen at the time and she could tell that the incident still haunted him. But even if he told her that he'd been acting out, how could she be certain it was the truth?

The sudden slamming of a door and the sound of Lane's truck's powerful engine starting caused her eyes to burn with unshed tears. He was doing what she wanted, so why did she feel so miserable about it?

But when she watched the taillights of his truck fade into the darkness as he drove away from the ranch toward the main highway, she couldn't hold back her emotions any longer. Tears ran unchecked down her cheeks as the only man she could ever love drove away from her.

"I'm staying here with you for a few days," Lane announced two hours later when T.J. opened his front door.

"Uh-oh. Something tells me there's trouble in paradise," T.J. said, standing back for Lane to enter the house. "What did you do?"

"What makes you think I did something?" Lane demanded.

"We're guys," T.J. answered. "We screw up all the time and women just love to point that out. So what did you do?"

"I don't want to talk about it," Lane ground out. The last thing he wanted to do was rehash what had taken place with Taylor. The woman was as stubborn and frustrating as a green-broke mule and his gut still burned with anger from their encounter.

"Let's go into the man cave," his brother said, nodding. "You look like you could use a drink."

"That's a given," Lane muttered, following his brother to the back of the house.

When they entered T.J.'s game room —decorated to look like an old-time saloon—Lane took a seat on one of the stools while his brother went behind the bar to get their beers. Lane stared at the miserable-looking man in the huge mirror on the wall behind the bar. He looked like hell. For that matter, he felt like it, too.

"So are you going to tell me or am I going to have to drag it out of you by playing twenty questions?" T.J. asked, breaking the silence.

Lane drained the bottle in his hand and just as he'd anticipated, his brother set him up with another one. "There's nothing to tell. She's pissed off and I'm staying with you. End of story."

"Well, you know I'd be the last one to pry into your personal business," T.J. said, as if choosing his words carefully.

"Since when?" Lane asked. "You've been the nosiest one of the six of us for as long as I've known you."

T.J. grinned. "It's something I'm good at. And I've always been of the opinion that if a person is good at something, they should do it often."

"This is one time you need to back off, brother," Lane warned. "I'm not in the mood and I'd hate to have to kick your ass."

"That must have been some argument," T.J. said, shaking his head. "You're usually the cool, calm and collected one of the bunch."

"Not tonight." Lane finished his beer. "I'll take another one."

T.J. got him another beer and set it in front of him. "You must really have it bad for Taylor if she's got you this tied up in knots." He frowned. "I don't think I've ever seen you drink that many beers so fast."

"Well, you might see me drink four or five more before it's over with." Maybe if he drank himself into oblivion he would find some peace from the burning ache that went all the way to his soul.

"She found out about your past, didn't she?" T.J. guessed.

Glaring at his brother, Lane took a swig of beer. "Shut up, T.J."

"How did she find out?" T.J. pressed.

"I don't know." Lane shook his head. "She didn't tell me and I didn't ask. Hell, it doesn't matter. She found out before I could tell her myself and jumped to the conclusion that I cheated her grandfather out of half of the Lucky Ace."

T.J. whistled low. "Even I've got better sense than to joke about you cheating at poker, let alone openly accuse you of doing it."

Nodding, Lane finished his beer and stood up. "Which room do you want me to take?"

"I've got six spare bedrooms," T.J. said, following him toward the stairs. "Take your pick."

As he climbed the steps to the upper floor, he knew

as surely as the sun set in the west each night that T.J. was already dialing the phone to let their other four brothers know what was going on. But it was the first time the phone tree of sympathy had been activated because of him. And he didn't like it one damned bit. He knew they would all be supportive and any advice they felt compelled to pass along would be out of concern for him. But he didn't want to hear it. Not tonight. Not tomorrow. Not ever.

Unfortunately, he didn't think there was anything they could do or say that would make the situation better anyway. Taylor had her mind made up and until she calmed down, the devil would be passing out ice water in hell before she listened to reason.

She'd been the same way about playing poker for the Lucky Ace. When he had learned that she didn't know the first thing about poker, he'd tried to call off the game, but she wouldn't hear of it. She had made up her mind that she could beat him and that was what she was determined to do. Dammit! The woman was way too stubborn for her own good.

Letting himself into the first bedroom he came to, Lane dropped his duffel bag on the floor, stripped off his clothes and headed straight for the shower. As he stood beneath the steamy spray, he closed his eyes and forced himself to put things into perspective. If he didn't love her so damned much, he might be tempted to throw up his hands and call it quits. She overreacted to just about everything and when she believed she was right about something, she was as determined to see it through as a dog fighting over a juicy ham bone.

But it was that very passion that he loved the most about her. When she committed herself to something, she gave it 150 percent, whether it was cooking a gourmet meal or making love with him.

Turning off the water, he grabbed a towel and dried himself off. She might have won tonight's hand, but he knew something about himself that she obviously didn't. He could be every bit as stubborn as she was and he wasn't about to give up on them so easily.

When he walked into the bedroom to stretch out on the bed, he stared at the ceiling. Even though he was still stinging from her lack of faith in him, he couldn't stay angry with her. He could understand how the evidence against him had to have looked to her. Considering his history and the fact that he hadn't told her about his past up front, he had to admit that it probably did appear that he had swindled her grandfather. Added to Taylor's tendency to jump to conclusions, it would have taken a miracle for her not to find him guilty of everything she had first suspected him of doing.

As he lay there thinking about how much he loved her and trying desperately to come up with a way he could make things right between them, a plan started to take shape. He knew exactly what he could do to convince her of his sincerity and control the outcome of the insane situation they found themselves in. And there wasn't a doubt in his mind that he was going to get what he wanted.

Folding his arms behind his head, Lane smiled determinedly. He hadn't expected to fall in love with her, had even tried to deny it was happening, but he was all in. He was going to do whatever it took to make her see they belonged together and she was just going to have to get used to it.

Nine

On Friday, when Lane arrived at the End of the Rainbow Casino, he went straight to Cole Sullivan's private office. "Is everything ready for the game?" he asked.

"It's good to see you again, Lane," the casino manager said, rising to his feet to shake Lane's hand. "The VIP room is ready and I have a dealer waiting to start the game as soon as Ms. Scott shows up."

"Good." Lane couldn't wait to get started. The sooner they settled control of the ranch, the sooner he could sort out matters once and for all with Taylor.

"How have you been?" Cole asked as he pulled an envelope from his desk drawer.

"Pretty good," Lane answered, checking his watch.

He hadn't seen or talked to Taylor for the past several days and it felt more like they'd been apart for years. He missed her, missed holding her and making love to her.

After he had gone to T.J.'s the night Taylor had confronted him with his past, he'd spent the next three days coming up with a plan of action and how he intended to execute it. He wanted to talk to her, needed to hear her voice. He had even picked up the phone a couple of times and started to call her, but he'd decided against it for one very important reason: what he wanted to say to her wasn't something a man told the woman he loved over the phone.

"I have this letter Ben left with me just before he went to California last fall," Cole said slowly, interrupting Lane's thoughts. "I was instructed to give it to both of you together. Would you like to see it before or after the game?"

"After," Lane said decisively. "It might be upsetting for Ms. Scott and I'd rather not have either of us distracted by whatever it says."

His friend nodded. "Can't say that I blame you." Cole paused a moment, then went on as he tucked the envelope into the inside pocket of his suit jacket. "I was left with the impression that Ben knew he wasn't going to make it back from his trip to California and he wanted to be sure the two of you were clear about his last wishes."

Lane couldn't imagine why Ben had included him in something that should have been a personal letter to his granddaughter. But then, there were a lot of things that Lane hadn't understood about the man. He knew for certain that Ben had had more than enough money on hand to cover his wager last fall. But instead of betting the cash, Ben had chosen to put up half of the Lucky

Ace. It hadn't made sense then and it didn't make any more sense to Lane now.

"Ms. Scott has arrived," Cole's secretary said through the intercom.

"Mr. Donaldson and I will be right out," Cole answered. He looked at Lane. "Are you ready to get this show on the road?"

Rising to his feet, Lane nodded. "The sooner the better."

As they walked out of the office into the reception area, he immediately spotted Taylor, sitting poised on the edge of a chair as if she was ready to bolt for the door. She looked nervous and if the dark circles under her eyes were any indication, she hadn't been sleeping any better than he had. But God, she looked good to him. It was all he could do to keep from crossing the room to take her in his arms.

"Taylor," he said, touching the wide brim of his hat and giving her a nod.

"Hello, Lane," she said, her tone cool.

An awkward silence followed until Cole cleared his throat. "If the two of you are ready, I'll show you to the VIP room and you can get started with your game," he announced.

As they followed the casino owner through the main floor to the private room, Lane gave her a sideways glance. "Are you doing all right?"

Staring straight ahead, she nodded. "Couldn't be better."

Her false bravado made him want to give her a hug of encouragement. He managed to resist. She wouldn't welcome the gesture and he wasn't sure he would be able to keep it friendly. What he really wanted to do was pick her up and carry her off to some place private where she would have to listen to his explanation—before he kissed her until they both collapsed from lack of oxygen.

When they entered the room, he held her chair for her to seat herself before he found his own place across the table from her. "Good luck, Taylor," he said, smiling.

"As you told me when you taught me how to play, luck has nothing to do with it," she said, throwing his words back at him. "Whoever has the better playing skills will decide the outcome of the game."

"But even highly skilled players make mistakes," he advised. "That's when you need to give your opponent the benefit of the doubt." He wasn't talking about playing poker and he could tell from the slight widening of her eyes that she knew it.

As they continued to stare at each other, Cole spoke up. "Edward will be your dealer today. There will be a five-minute break every hour until the game is finished. I'll be the observer and verify the results of the game." Taking his seat at the table to watch them play, the man added, "Good luck to both of you."

Lane knew the game wouldn't take long enough for them to reach the first break. He had a plan and as soon as he knew he held the winning hand, he intended to execute it.

Fifteen minutes later, he glanced at the hold cards he'd just been dealt, then at the three flop cards lying faceup on the table. The moment he had been waiting for had arrived.

"Your bet, Taylor," he said, calmly.

Watching for the slightest show of one of her tells, he knew immediately when she hesitated with her bet that she was calculating the odds of her having the winning hand. It was all he could do to keep from smiling.

When she placed a small bet, she smiled. "Your turn."

"All in," he said, shoving his entire stack of chips into the pot. He had won more chips than she had, but that was part of his plan. If she matched his bet, it would set her up for the game to be over with the next hand.

As he watched her, Lane was proud that Taylor wasn't nibbling on her lower lip as she tried to decide if she should match his bet. But from the cards he held and the cards showing on the table, he knew she had nothing to worry about. "All in," she finally said, shoving all of her chips into the pot.

He could tell she was more than a little apprehensive by the slight quiver in her voice. Nothing would have pleased him more than to take her in his arms and kiss her nervousness away.

They both turned over their hold cards as they waited for the dealer to reveal the last two community cards. He had a pair of nines, while she had a possible straight.

His heart thumped hard against his ribs as Edward dealt the turn card and then the river card face up. Thankfully, they were of no help to him, but she did end up with the straight she was hoping for. "I thought my pair had you beat," he said, hoping that he looked and sounded convincing.

For the first time since sitting down at the table, she smiled at him. "Apparently not," she said as the dealer raked her chips and most of Lane's to her side of the table.

Left with just enough chips to make his play convincing, Lane waited until the dealer finished dealing the flop before he looked at his hold cards. When he did, he almost groaned aloud. He had a pair of kings and odds were she had a lesser hand. He could only hope that she beat him with the community cards.

Placing his bet, he shoved all but one chip into the pot. "As long as I have a chip and a chair, I have a chance," he said, smiling. When she hesitated, he held his breath. It would have been much easier to fold if he'd been dealt cards he knew would lose. But as he stared at her across the table, he knew his choice was the easiest one he'd ever made. Taylor thought they were playing for the ranch. But he knew there was much more at stake than a thousand acres of Texas dirt. And for the first time in his life, he was going to throw a game and hope that it was enough to get what he wanted.

"I'll match that bet," she said decisively and without hesitation.

The dealer dealt the flop—two tens and a king. Lane's heart felt as though it would jump out of his chest. He had a full house. Why the hell couldn't she have gotten his hand?

The competitor in him wanted to play the cards and

win. But as he stared at her across the table, his heart told him he had only one choice.

Taking a deep breath, he shook his head. "I fold," he said, leaving his hold cards face down as he conceded the game and picked up his remaining chip. "You win, Taylor."

Lane ignored the startled look on Cole Sullivan's face as he stood up and offered to shake her hand. "Congratulations. The Lucky Ace is yours and yours alone." When she placed her small hand in his, it felt as if a jolt of electric current passed between them. He'd done the right thing—the only thing he could do. He only hoped his plan worked and it wasn't the last time he would be allowed to touch her.

"It was a good game and you played quite well. I'm proud of you, Taylor."

"I had a good teacher," she said softly. The sadness in her emerald eyes was almost his undoing.

"Enjoy the ranch," he said as he slipped the poker chip into his jeans pocket and turned toward the door.

Forcing himself to move before he changed his mind, Lane walked away without so much as a backward glance and headed for the casino exit, leaving the only woman he would ever love behind.

Saddling Cinnamon, Taylor mounted the buckskin mare and headed south toward the creek. Her emotions were a tangled mess and she didn't see how she could feel any worse. Hopefully she could think more clearly and somehow draw strength from the place where she and her grandfather had gone fishing so many times.

The place where he had asked her grandmother to marry him. The same place she and Lane had picnicked the day they went riding.

Her confused feelings had begun the night she confronted him with what she had learned about his past and had only gotten worse this afternoon after Lane had walked out of the poker room. She knew it was a rule that once a player folded his cards, they were dead and other players weren't supposed to look at them, but she hadn't cared. Her instincts had told her that beating Lane shouldn't have been that easy. And she'd been right. He'd folded a full house, which would have easily beaten her three of a kind.

Why had he done that? Why had he thrown the game and given her his share of the Lucky Ace? And why did finally having all of the ranch make her feel as if she was the one who'd lost more than she had gained?

When she reached the creek, she dismounted and ground tied the mare. Walking over to the creek bank, she lowered herself to the grass and took the letter from the pocket of her jeans. Cole Sullivan had given it to her just before she left the casino, but she hadn't read it yet. On the front of it her grandfather had written both her name and Lane's. But she had no idea if or when she would ever see Lane again.

She closed her eyes and took several deep breaths. Just the thought of never seeing him again, never being held by him or having him love her so tenderly, caused tears to spill down her cheeks. She loved him more than she had ever dreamed she would love anyone and she'd driven him away.

The night she had ordered him off the ranch, Lane had been right—she did tend to overreact and refuse to listen when someone tried to explain things to her.

Taylor opened her eyes to stare at the crystal-clear water in the creek. The day after Lane left the Lucky Ace, she had realized that she should have given him a chance to explain. But she had thought there would be time after the ownership of the ranch was decided to apologize and tell him she was ready to hear his explanation. Unfortunately, he had walked out of the casino before she'd had the chance.

Now she didn't even know where he was. She supposed she could call one of his brothers to find out where he had gone and how to get in touch with him. But she'd decided against that. She wasn't comfortable with getting his family involved. For one thing, she wasn't certain they would tell her. And for another, she wasn't like her parents. She would prefer to keep her and Lane's differences private. A sudden thought caused her to suck in a sharp breath. Was she repeating the mistakes of her parents? Feeling more miserable by the second, she realized that was exactly what she had done. Her mother and father always overreacted to the slightest problem and were both too stubborn to listen to reason. That's why their differences always escalated into shouting matches.

But Lane had refused to lower himself to that level. He had remained calm and tried to discuss the issues she had with him in a reasonable manner, even though she could tell he had been furious about her accusations.

Needing a distraction from her disturbing self-discovery, she swiped at her eyes with the back of her hand, broke the seal and opened the flap of the envelope. When she removed the folded sheet of paper, she recognized her grandfather's handwriting immediately, causing a fresh wave of tears to flow down her cheeks.

Finally managing to bring herself back under control, she felt worse than ever as she read his message. Lane had been telling her the truth all along. He hadn't cheated to win the game he'd played with her grandfather. Ben Cunningham had thrown the game in order for Lane and Taylor to meet.

As she read on, Taylor was amazed at the lengths her grandfather had gone to in playing matchmaker. He had choreographed the entire ranch ownership fiasco. From his request that Lane move into the ranch house to telling her that he wanted her to leave California and live on the Lucky Ace, her grandfather had set them up because he felt they would be a good match—much like he and her grandmother had been.

Taylor wasn't sure how long she sat on the creek bank staring at the slow moving water, but a rustling sound caused her to turn and look behind her. Lane had ground tied his gelding beside her mare and was walking toward her. She'd been so lost in her misery she hadn't even heard him ride up.

Her heart skipped several beats just from the sight of him. In the black jeans, white dress shirt and black Western-cut sports jacket he had worn for their poker game, he had looked good to her. But now, dressed in his worn blue jeans, a chambray shirt and black leather vest, Lane couldn't have looked more handsome. He looked like the cowboy she had come to know over the past several weeks—the man she had come to love more than life itself.

"When I didn't find you at the house, I figured you might be here," he said, lowering himself onto the grass beside her.

"What are you doing here, Lane?" she asked. She hadn't meant to be so blunt, but after the way she had acted the night she had ordered him off the ranch, she was having a hard time believing he would even want to see her, let alone take the time to search for her.

"I stopped by to bring the papers Ben and I signed when I won half of the ranch," he said, taking some folded documents from the inside of his black leather vest.

He looked so good to her and nothing would please her more than having him take her into his arms and tell her that everything was going to work out. But she knew that was never going to happen—not after the accusations she'd made.

"I—I forgot there would be legal papers to sign," she said, barely resisting the urge to reach out and touch his lean cheek.

She watched him turn the documents over in his hands as he stared down at them. "Before I give these to you, I want you to listen to what I have to say," he said slowly. "And I'd really like for you to hear me out before you comment."

"All right." She nodded. "I have something I need to say to you, too." Admitting that she had been wrong wasn't easy for her, but she owed him an apology for accusing him of swindling her grandfather, as well as overreacting when she discovered the truth about his past.

He took a deep breath, then raising his gaze to meet hers, he shook his head. "I wasn't trying to hide what I did when I was a kid," he said. "It's not something I'm proud of and I prefer not to think about it, but I did intend to tell you about it at some point."

"After the things I had accused you of the night I arrived, I can understand your reluctance." She had unknowingly brought up his past that night and given her insistence that he was guilty, she couldn't blame him for being hesitant about sharing his youthful mistakes.

He shrugged. "I don't know how much you know about it, but my dad embezzled a fortune from the people who trusted him to build their savings. That's why he took his own life. He knew he was facing the rest of his years in prison and he wasn't man enough to face the consequences of his actions."

"I read about your father's crimes in the article from one of the Houston papers," she admitted.

"My mom wasn't aware of what he had been doing, but by the time he died, my father had squandered all of their savings, as well as run through millions of his clients' money." He stared off into the distance. "I'm not sure why he did it, but I suspect he was trying to project an image of being a huge success."

"He might have thought it was important for the type of job he had," she suggested gently.

"Probably." Lane shook his head. "Anyway, after he died my mom found a job as a receptionist in a big corporate office and we had to move out of the suburbs and into an apartment in Houston because we didn't have a car. Both of our vehicles were sold along with everything else at the court-ordered auction."

"That had to have been a huge adjustment for you and your mom." She could only imagine how hard that had been for both of them.

He nodded. "Everything was going along okay and we were squeaking by until my mom found a lump in her breast." His expression hardened. "Because of the treatments she needed, she couldn't work, and along with losing her job, she lost her health insurance."

"That has happened to a lot of people," she said, thinking how unfair it all was. "How old were you?"

"I was fourteen and suddenly thrust into the role of being our sole means of support," he said, taking a deep breath.

"Couldn't your mother apply for assistance from some of the state agencies?" she asked.

"She did," he admitted. "But they had a backlog of cases and we needed money right then." He gave her a meaningful look. "Some landlords don't give a damn what people are going through. They want their money when the rent is due or they'll toss you out in the street. Same thing goes for grocery stores. If you don't pay for the food, you don't eat."

"I'm so sorry for what you had to go through," she said, feeling worse than ever. When she found out about his past, she had assumed he stole things for the fun of it or had been rebelling as a lot of teenagers do. But that hadn't been the case. Lane had turned to crime as a way to survive.

"I wasn't old enough to get a real job and it didn't take long for me to figure out that mowing lawns and doing odd jobs wasn't cutting it," he continued. "I had to find a way to make some real money."

"That's when you started—"

"Yeah, that's when I became a thief," he interrupted. "I stole whatever I thought I could resell, went door-to-door selling magazine subscriptions that people were never going to get and solicited donations for charities that didn't exist. I did whatever I could think of to make ends meet."

"Did your mother know?" Taylor asked, her heart breaking for what he'd had to do.

"If she did, she was too sick to care," Lane answered. He glanced down at his hands. "She died six months after her diagnosis and it wasn't long after that I was caught trying to sell an expensive silver tray to a pawn dealer."

"Is that when you became a ward of the state?" she asked.

He nodded. "When my case came up in court, the judge looked at the evidence against me, and after asking me why I had done the things I had done, he took pity on me. He said that if I pleaded guilty to the charges, instead of a juvenile detention center, I would be put into the foster care system and sent to the Last Chance Ranch." Looking directly at her, he smiled. "That was the best thing that ever happened to me."

"That's when you met your brothers," she said,

knowing how important they had become to each other. The Last Chance Ranch had saved him and enriched his life in so many ways.… She was just beginning to understand why he wanted to own part of the Lucky Ace.

"Yes." Lane reached out and took her hand in his. "I gained siblings and a dad who took the time and cared enough to help me move past what had happened." His tone changed to one of fondness. "Hank Calvert had his hands full with the six of us. But he used ranch work and rodeo competitions to keep us busy and help us work off some of the anger we had to deal with." Chuckling, he added, "And the words of wisdom he passed along were priceless."

"What did he tell you?" she asked, loving the way her hand felt in his.

"Oh, things like being polite and dusting your hand off on the seat of your jeans before you shake hands with somebody," he said, grinning. "Then there was the lecture every time one of us had a date about how to treat a lady. If I heard 'don't forget to open her doors' once, I heard it a thousand times." Laughing, he added, "Another one he was particularly fond of telling us was, 'unless your arms are broke, you'd better carry whatever it is she needs carrying.'"

"Is that the reason you always hold my chair when I sit down?" she asked, smiling back at him.

"Yup." His grin widened. "Hank had a laundry list of things he said made a man into a real man. He called it the Cowboy Code, and I can honestly say he lived by everything on that list."

"He sounds like he was a wonderful man," Taylor

said, wishing she could have met the cowboy who had cared enough to help boys who might otherwise have continued down the wrong path in life.

"He sure was," Lane said fondly.

"Lane, I'm sorry for all those awful things I said to you the other night," she said, feeling horrible about her accusations. "I should have let you explain everything instead of demanding that you leave. I really need to work on controlling my tendency to jump to conclusions and overreact first without listening to reason."

He nodded. "You're a very passionate woman."

"That's no excuse for my behavior," she insisted. "Please accept my apology."

"Don't worry, Taylor," he said, his smile sending shivers up her spine. "All is forgiven."

They sat in silence for several long moments before she asked, "Lane, why did you fold your hand today? You had me beat and we both know it."

When his dark brown gaze met hers, her heart skipped a beat. "I knew that you wanted all of the Lucky Ace." With her hand still in his, he gave it a little squeeze. "And I realized that you and your happiness were more important to me than a thousand acres of Texas dust."

"Lane, I—"

Placing his index finger to her lips, he shook his head. "You said you'd listen to me." He replaced his finger with his lips to give her a kiss that robbed her of breath. "I have another business proposal I'd like to run past you."

"Okay." His kiss felt wonderful and having spent

four days without it, she wanted more. "What do you have in mind?"

"I was thinking that if you don't mind, I could stay here for a while and help you run the ranch," he offered. "Do you think that's something you would be interested in?"

Hope began to rise within her. "Yes, I would really like that."

He gave a short nod. "And what would you say to me living in the house with you?"

"That would be nice," she said as her pulse sped up.

"How would you feel about having the master bedroom remodeled and redecorated?" he asked, looking thoughtful. "Is that something you would be open to doing?"

"That would be a good idea," she said, nodding.

He seemed to consider her answer for a moment before he asked, "After it's redecorated, would you be open to making it your bedroom?"

"I suppose that I should," she said, wondering where he was going with his suggestions.

"And if I promise not to snore too loud, would you be open to me staying in there with you?" he asked, raising their entwined hands to his lips to kiss the back of her hand.

"I would love that," she said, meaning it. She started to move closer to him, but he raised his hand to stop her.

"Just wait," he said. "You haven't heard the rest of my proposal."

"All right, you have my attention," she said, grinning. He was going to stay at the Lucky Ace. That's all she cared about.

"Would you be willing to sign a document that states I have the right to live here with you on your ranch?" he asked.

She frowned. "I guess that would be all right."

"I would want witnesses," he warned.

"I think most legal agreements are witnessed," she said, nodding.

When he pulled her into his arms, the feeling of once again being held by the man she loved brought tears to her eyes. "How would you feel about changing your name?" he asked, his handsome face breaking into a grin that sent her heart soaring. "Or maybe hyphenating it."

"What are you asking?" she asked, unable to draw in enough air.

"I love you, Taylor, and I'm asking you to marry me," he said, the light in his eyes reflecting a love she had never dreamed possible. He handed her the poker chip he had picked up before he left the casino in Shreveport. "I want you to keep this and every time you look at it, I want you to know that you're the woman who inspired me to give up my professional playing status."

"You mean it?" she asked. "I'm the woman who tempted you to quit playing? And you're willing to put up with me and the way I jump to conclusions and overreact?"

"Your passion is one of the things I love about you, babe," he said, kissing her until they both gasped for breath.

"And you really love me?" she asked, afraid to believe it was true.

"More than life itself," he said without hesitation. "Now, are you going to keep me waiting with your answer, or are you going to tell me you love me, too, and that you would be happy to be my wife?"

"Yes, I love you," she said, kissing him. "Yes, I'll marry you. And yes, I want to sleep in the master suite with you every night for the rest of our lives."

"Thank God!" His arms tightened around her as if he never intended to let her go. "When do you want to get married, Taylor?"

"Whenever you do," she said, happier than she'd ever been in her entire life.

"As far as I'm concerned, I'd like to make you mine as soon as we can get a marriage license," he said, kissing her again. "But I'm sure you'd like a wedding, and that takes time to plan."

"I'd like for my parents to be here," she agreed. Even though they fought constantly, she loved them and they loved her. Surely they could put their differences aside for one day.

"Why don't we go back to the house?" he asked, standing up, then helping her to her feet. "The sooner we get started on those wedding plans, the sooner we can get married and start working on a full house."

She laughed. "How many children do you want?"

"I don't want any for a while," he said, putting his arm around her as they walked over to the horses. "I want to spend some time just being me and you. But when we do start having kids, I can guarantee you that I'll be more than happy to give you all you want."

"Oh, I almost forgot to show you the letter from my grandfather," she said as they mounted the horses and started across the pasture.

"I'll look at it later," he said, giving her a smile that lit the darkest corners of her soul. "Right now, I want to get home and make love to the hottest woman I've ever met."

"I love you, Lane Donaldson."

"And I love you, babe. More than you'll ever know."

"I think we've settled the matter of whether the Lucky Ace is your ranch or mine," she said thoughtfully as they mounted their horses.

"We did that when we played that poker game today," he said, grinning. "It's yours."

Shaking her head, she grinned back at the man she loved with all her heart and soul. "No, Lane. The Lucky Ace belongs to both of us. It's *our* ranch."

Epilogue

"Who won the pool about me and Taylor getting married?" Lane asked his brothers as he watched his beautiful wife join in the line dancing with Bria, Summer and Mariah. She was the most gorgeous woman he had ever seen and he couldn't believe she had agreed to become his wife.

"I took this one," T.J. spoke up, grinning from ear to ear. "I said it would be the fourth of July."

"How much longer before the fireworks start?" Nate asked, checking his watch. "I have a phone call to make."

"You have about an hour," Lane said, eyeing his brother. "You got a new woman on the string?"

"Something like that," Nate said evasively as he took his cell phone from his pocket. "I think I'll go make that call now. I should be back in plenty of time for the fireworks."

"Who's the lucky lady?" Ryder asked when Nate strolled off with his phone to his ear.

"He and that little blonde down in Waco are talking again," Jaron answered, sounding distracted.

Lane noticed that Jaron hadn't taken his eyes off of Mariah since he'd arrived for the wedding. "Still haven't changed your mind about being too old for her?" Lane asked, taking a swig of his beer.

Jaron shrugged. "Nope."

"You're hopeless," Ryder said disgustedly as he shifted little Katie to his shoulder.

"You could at least ask her to dance," Sam pointed out.

Jaron shook his head. "No sense starting something I don't intend to finish."

"Damn, but you're a stubborn cuss," T.J. said, laughing.

"And you're full of bull," Jaron shot back. "What's your point?"

"So who's going to be the next brother to take the plunge?" Lane asked, smiling at his new bride when she lifted her wedding gown to do a series of dance steps, revealing a pair of white cowgirl boots. He couldn't wait for the reception to wind down so he could spirit her away for their first night as husband and wife.

"Not me," T.J. said, shaking his head. "I'm a confirmed bachelor and likely to remain so."

"You mean you haven't cozied up to your neighbor?" Sam asked, grinning. "Now that her stallion is staying on his side of the fence, I thought the two of you were getting along better."

"Not even on a bet," T.J. said vehemently. "I like her just fine as long as she stays on her side of the fence and I stay on mine and I don't have to deal with her. She's the kind of trouble I don't want or need."

"I think he's protesting just a little too much, don't you guys?" Lane teased.

"I think you're right," Sam agreed.

"I think you're both full of bull roar and buffalo chips," T.J. shot back. "My money is on Nate taking a trip down the aisle next."

"He does keep going back to the blonde in Waco," Ryder admitted.

While his brothers continued to speculate on which one would be the next to join the ranks of the blissfully hitched, Lane set his beer bottle on a table and walked over to the band. After making his request, he waited until they struck up the first chords of the song before he crooked his finger at Taylor. Looking like an angel in her full-length wedding gown, she smiled and floated across the dance floor toward him.

"I'd really like to dance with you, Mrs. Donaldson," he said, smiling as he took her in his arms.

"I love the way my new name sounds," she said, putting her arms around his neck.

"Donaldson?" he asked, raising an eyebrow.

She laughed. "No. The Mrs. part."

"How much longer before we can leave?" he asked, hoping she agreed to their departure sooner rather than later.

"I'm ready now," she said, kissing his chin. "The dinner is over with, we've cut the cake and we've danced. I'd call that good."

"As soon as this dance is over, we're out of here," he said, unable to stop grinning.

"Oh, my word, Mr. Donaldson," she teased. "You're giving away your tell. From the look on your face, I know exactly what you're thinking."

Laughing, he nodded. "I guess I'll have to work on hiding that."

"Don't you dare," she whispered, sending a wave of heat from the top of his head to the soles of his feet. "I like knowing that you want me as much as I want you."

His body tightened to an almost painful state and to get his mind off what they would be doing later, he nodded toward her parents, dancing just a few feet away. "Your folks seem to be getting along pretty well."

"I know." She smiled. "I've never seen them this relaxed. They actually seem pretty happy tonight."

When the song finally ended, Lane took her by the hand, led her across the dance floor and straight to the house, waving to his brothers as they walked past them. He held her hand as they climbed the stairs, then stopped at the door with the poker chip he'd given her attached to it—the door to the master suite.

"I've been wanting to make love to you in this bedroom ever since it was finished," he said, picking her up to carry her across the threshold of their newly decorated room. They had agreed to wait to make love in their new bedroom until after they were man and wife.

"Oh, I forgot about the fireworks," Taylor said when

he started to unbutton the tiny buttons at the back of her wedding gown.

"Don't worry about it, babe," he said, giving her a kiss filled with all of the love in his heart. "We'll make some fireworks of our own."

And as the night sky outside their bedroom window was lit by an array of colored starbursts, they did just that.

* * * * *

If you loved Lane's story,
pick up the other novels in
USA TODAY *bestselling author*
Kathie DeNosky's
THE GOOD, THE BAD AND THE TEXAN,
a series about six foster brothers from the
Last Chance Ranch!

HIS MARRIAGE TO REMEMBER
A BABY BETWEEN FRIENDS

Both available now from Harlequin Desire!

REQUEST YOUR FREE BOOKS!
2 FREE NOVELS PLUS 2 FREE GIFTS!

HARLEQUIN® *Desire*

ALWAYS POWERFUL, PASSIONATE AND PROVOCATIVE

YES! Please send me 2 FREE Harlequin Desire® novels and my 2 FREE gifts (gifts are worth about $10). After receiving them, if I don't wish to receive any more books, I can return the shipping statement marked "cancel." If I don't cancel, I will receive 6 brand-new novels every month and be billed just $4.55 per book in the U.S. or $4.99 per book in Canada. That's a savings of at least 13% off the cover price! It's quite a bargain! Shipping and handling is just 50¢ per book in the U.S. and 75¢ per book in Canada.* I understand that accepting the 2 free books and gifts places me under no obligation to buy anything. I can always return a shipment and cancel at any time. Even if I never buy another book, the two free books and gifts are mine to keep forever.

225/326 HDN F4ZC

Name	(PLEASE PRINT)

Address	Apt. #

City	State/Prov.	Zip/Postal Code

Signature (if under 18, a parent or guardian must sign)

Mail to the **Harlequin®** Reader Service:

IN U.S.A.: P.O. Box 1867, Buffalo, NY 14240-1867
IN CANADA: P.O. Box 609, Fort Erie, Ontario L2A 5X3

Want to try two free books from another line?
Call 1-800-873-8635 or visit www.ReaderService.com.

* Terms and prices subject to change without notice. Prices do not include applicable taxes. Sales tax applicable in N.Y. Canadian residents will be charged applicable taxes. Offer not valid in Quebec. This offer is limited to one order per household. Not valid for current subscribers to Harlequin Desire books. All orders subject to credit approval. Credit or debit balances in a customer's account(s) may be offset by any other outstanding balance owed by or to the customer. Please allow 4 to 6 weeks for delivery. Offer available while quantities last.

Your Privacy—The Harlequin® Reader Service is committed to protecting your privacy. Our Privacy Policy is available online at www.ReaderService.com or upon request from the Harlequin Reader Service.

We make a portion of our mailing list available to reputable third parties that offer products we believe may interest you. If you prefer that we not exchange your name with third parties, or if you wish to clarify or modify your communication preferences, please visit us at www.ReaderService.com/consumerchoice or write to us at Harlequin Reader Service Preference Service, P.O. Box 9062, Buffalo, NY 14269. Include your complete name and address.

HDI3R

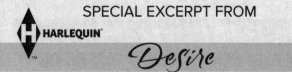

SPECIAL EXCERPT FROM

HARLEQUIN

Desire

Read on for a sneak peek at USA TODAY *bestselling author*
Yvonne Lindsay's EXPECTING THE CEO'S CHILD,
the third novel in Harlequin Desire's
DYNASTIES: THE LASSITERS *series.*

CEO restaurateur Dylan Lassiter is in for a big surprise from
a fling he can't forget…

The sound of the door buzzer alerted Jenna to a customer out front. She pasted a smile on her face and walked out into the showroom only to feel the smile freeze in place as she recognized Dylan Lassiter, in all his decadent glory, standing with his back to her, his attention apparently captured by the ready-made bouquets she kept in the refrigerated unit along one wall.

Her reaction was instantaneous—heat, desire and shock each flooded her in turn. The last time she'd seen him had been in the coat closet where they'd impulsively sought refuge, releasing the sexual energy that had ignited so dangerously and suddenly between them.

"Can I help you?" she asked, feigning a lack of recognition right up until the moment he turned around and impaled her with those cerulean-blue eyes of his.

Her mouth dried. It was a crime against nature that any man could look so beautiful and so masculine all at the same time.

A hank of softly curling hair fell across his high forehead, making her hand itch to smooth it back, to then trace the stubbled line of his jaw.

She'd spent the past two and a half months in a state of disbelief at her actions. It had literally been a one-night *stand*, she reminded herself cynically. The coat closet hadn't allowed for anything else. Her body still remembered every second of how he'd made her feel—and reacted in kind again.

"Jenna," Dylan acknowledged with a slow nod of his head, his gaze not moving from her face for a second.

"Dylan," she said, feigning surprise. "What brings you back to Cheyenne?"

The instant she said the words she silently groaned. Of course he was here for the opening of his new restaurant. The local chamber of commerce—heck, the whole town—was abuzz with the news. She'd tried to ignore anything Lassiter-related for weeks now, but there was no ignoring the man in front of her.

The father of her unborn child.

Don't miss EXPECTING THE CEO'S CHILD
by Yvonne Lindsay, available June 2014.

Wherever Harlequin® Desire
books and ebooks are sold.

HARLEQUIN®

Desire

ALWAYS POWERFUL, PASSIONATE AND PROVOCATIVE.

BABY FOR KEEPS
Billionaires and Babies
by Janice Maynard

"I have a proposition for you."

Wealthy Dylan Kavanagh loves being a hero, so when single
mom Mia needs help, Dylan offers her a room—at his place.
But close proximity soon has Dylan thinking about making
this little family his—for keeps.

Look for
BABY FOR KEEPS
in June 2014, from Harlequin® Desire!
Wherever books and ebooks are sold.

Don't miss other scandalous titles from the
Billionaires and Babies miniseries,
available now wherever books and ebooks are sold.

Billionaires and Babies: Powerful men…wrapped around their
babies' little fingers